MURDER AT DEVIL'S BRIDGE

KEIRON COSGRAVE

INDIUM

DEATH CAN COME IN THE MOST
BEAUTIFUL OF PLACES...

COPYRIGHT

www.keironcosgrave.net

Facebook: Keiron Cosgrave Author
Cover and Interior Design, Editor: Author
Publisher: Indium Books
Third Edition - May 2021(P)

Reader's note: This novel has been written in British English.

We operate a policy of continuous improvement. Every effort is made to minimise errors, typos, issues of grammar, etc. Occasionally, despite our best efforts, errors creep through. Reader feedback is actively encouraged and appreciated via the contact form on the website.

PROLOGUE

Saturday 5th August, 10:00 a.m.

Sheepwash Bridge, near Osmotherley, North Yorkshire

Brittle sun-scorched heather crunched under the soles of retired teacher Tony Mason's expensive Meindl walking boots. Low on the southern horizon, a long and languorous trail of grey smoke drifted into an unblemished pastel blue sky. A curlew's call echoed across the moor. Somewhere high on the updraft, a skylark sang like its life depended on it. From the east, a jet rumbled into Teesside Airport. Midges feasted on the heat.

A balmy August day getting hotter. Tony imagined red top headlines: *PHEW! WHAT A SCORCHER!*

Stepping off the moor, Tony started across the gravel car park towards the stone bridge spanning the beck. A cloud of dust rose into the air behind him.

Reaching the beck, he lowered his backpack to the ground and sat on the cool Yorkstone parapet with a long view down the valley. Batting midges, he drew a deep, invigorating breath and gulped water from a canteen. Half a mile distant, framed by pine woods, starbursts of sunlight glinted from the surface of Cod Beck Reservoir.

Two minutes of tranquil calm passed.

Tony glanced right and watched his two-year-old black Labrador, Coco, rush headlong into a stand of tall pines.

Hot and breathless, he wiped the sweat off of his forehead, reclaimed his backpack, collected a protein bar, unwrapped it and took a first bite. Finishing up, he stuffed the wrapper into the backpack, burped under a clenched fist and made to rise. Rising, straightening, vertebrae cracking, a speeding black dot caught in the corner of his right eye. Settling a flattened palm over his brow, he watched the dot increase in size and become identifiably, a fighter jet skimming the moor towards him at a rate of knots. As the plane closed in, captured by some giant invisible hand, Tony hunkered down. The low flying jet thundered past in a crescendo of sound, a blur of grey and shimmer of heat. Half a minute later, he lost sight of the jet over the horizon.

Silence returned to the valley, but for Coco nuzzling through the undergrowth.

Scanning the pines, Tony caught sight of Coco sniffing and pawing at the base of a mound of stone. He called out. Coco, untroubled, continued to paw.

'Bloody animal,' he grumbled, setting off at a march towards the dog.

Two metres distant from Coco, Tony stalled. The air was fragrant with the eye-watering stench of maggoty decay. It made him retch. Gagging, pinching his nostrils together, with a hand firm across his mouth, he inched forward and took Coco by the collar and dragged him away. Coming to fresher air, he tied Coco's lead around a tree trunk, stood back and pressed her hind quarters to the ground with a firm hand.

'Sit, girl, sit. What've you found, eh? Something nasty?' he said, turning to study the mound. 'A dead sheep is it? Poor thing got caught up in the branches, did it?'

Tony launched a kick at the mound with the sole of his right boot. The top layer of the mound loosened and fell into the ferns and revealed a rolled up grey, black-flecked rug, with a tasselled edge. Studying the rug, what remained of the mound, his brow furrowed into a frown. Curiosity aroused, he crouched down, took a firm grip of the tasselled edge and pulled hard. As he did so, the mound broke apart. He jumped back. An avalanche of stone cascaded down the hillside and splashed into the beck.

Returning his gaze to the mound, he felt something slump and settle against his ankles. He looked down, gazed at a corpse. A naked woman lay face down against his ankles with a foot-long, raggedy wound running diagonally across her shattered skull. Tidy ranks of rice-like bluebottle eggs marked the edges of the wound. Startled, Tony scrambled away, clipping the corpse with a heel. The corpse rocked, then sloughed flat. A flatulent hiss and the rank stench of death filled the air.

'What the..!' he exclaimed, untying Coco, setting off for car park. 'Come on, girl, we'd better make tracks. Sod's law, there's no bloody signal here. And I need to call 999.'

THE WEEK BEFORE

CHAPTER ONE

TUESDAY 1ST AUGUST, **9:00 p.m.**

Desk Sergeant Willie Thorne had taken it upon himself to prop open the double doors into the custody suite reception with timber wedges. A cool breeze ran through the space, providing welcome relief from the oppressive heat. The listless air was laced with a subtle concoction of vomit, sweat and cleaning fluids.

Commercial lawyer, Drew Tomlinson, marched into the custody suite, halted at the desk and said without preamble: 'I'd like to report a missing person.'

Willie looked up from the custody record and settled his reading glasses on his chest. 'Alright. And what, may I ask, sir, is your relationship to the missing person?'

'She's my wife.'

'OK. And your wife's name, sir?'

'Claire Emily Tomlinson. We spoke last early Sunday evening, in the driveway at home. She told me she was staying over a friend's house in Masham Monday night, returning home this afternoon. Said she'd be back by five this afternoon to take our daughter, Emily, to her ballet lesson. She didn't come home, and I haven't been able to raise her on her mobile. I'm very worried about her.'

'The Sunday just gone, sir?'

'That's right.'

'What time was this, sir? The last time you saw her?'

'It had just gone six. I remember it because the BBC News was starting; the theme tune was playing in the background as I waved her off from the door. She was at the wheel of her car. It's a silver BMW – a 420d.'

Thorne nodded, scribbled notes. 'I hope you don't mind me asking, sir, but did you think on to contact your wife's friend in Masham? Find out if she arrived? When she left?'

Annoyance flared in Drew's eyes, his jaw firmed, lips pursed. 'What do you take me for, Sergeant? Of course, I bloody have. I phoned earlier. I caught Sally as she was leaving work. She told me Claire never arrived on Sunday as planned. She's tried to contact Claire on her mobile. So far, she's had no joy. The thing is, Sergeant, Sally didn't have either our landline, or my mobile number. She only ever contacts Claire on her mobile.'

Thorne breathed in through his nose. 'So, what you're telling me is... Your wife's been missing for a little over forty-eight hours?'

'It would seem so, yes,'

'Mr Tomlinson. Take a seat. With luck, there will be a detective burning the midnight oil, upstairs. The Major Crime Unit are rushed off their feet at the moment. There's no rest for us bobbies. Not in modern Britain, there isn't.'

Tomlinson stepped back, said: 'Thank you. Is there somewhere I can buy a hot drink? I'm parched.'

Thorne shook his head. 'Sorry, no. I'll fetch a detective. I'm sure someone will put the kettle on, if you ask them nicely.'

Tomlinson nodded, smiled without conviction. Turning from the desk, he padded over to and lowered into a chair by the window. Sitting back, he rolled his eyes to the ceiling and massaged gritty eyes. After a minute, his eyelids stuttered closed.

Inside a minute, his snores rattled from the walls.

* * *

'Sir,' barked Thorne. 'Sir!'

'Ugh,' grumbled Tomlinson with a start. 'Where the hell am I?'

Thorne and Detective Sergeant David Watts exchanged frustrated glances.

'You're here, sir. Harrogate Police HQ. You came about your wife. Remember?' said Thorne, shrugging.

Pushing up in the chair, Tomlinson flicked sleep from the corner of his eyes. 'Sorry. I must have dozed off. It's been a long day.'

'You did. Mr Tomlinson, this is Detective Sergeant David Watts. He's here to talk to you about your wife.'

David Watts thrust out a hand. They shook hands. Tomlinson raised up, stood and tidied his shirt into the waistband of his trousers, adjusted his belt.

'Nice to meet you, Mr Tomlinson,' said Watts. 'Would you care to join me in an interview room?'

'That's why I'm here. Please, lead on.'

Watts set off along the corridor with Tomlinson in tow.

Once settled in the interview room, Watts said: 'I understand you came to report your wife as a missing person?'

A nod. A sniffle. 'Yes. I haven't seen or heard from Claire, for two days. She told me she was staying with a friend in

Masham from Sunday evening through to late this afternoon. We were planning to go out for an Italian tonight. The three of us were going; myself, Claire and Emily. Emily is our teenage daughter. Of course, that won't be happening now. I was looking forward to it, too. Their duck pasta in a Porcini mushroom sauce, with sautéed vegetables, is to die for. You ought to try it sometime.'

Where did that come from, thought Watts? *Some people...* 'For the record, sir. Your wife's friend, her name?'

'Sally Evans. She's one of Claire's uni pals. One of many. They like to stay in contact. Try to see meet up every couple of months. Sally runs a teashop in the village square in Masham. Claire lends a hand sometimes, if she's able to. She covers staff holidays. She says she loves meeting the customers. Claire is a stay-at-home mum, so it makes a pleasant change for her.'

Watts nodded. 'You told the Desk Sergeant Claire never arrived in Masham. Are you sure about that?'

Tomlinson shrugged. 'I'm only going on what Sally told me.'

'Any reason you didn't report your wife's disappearance to us, earlier, Mr Tomlinson? I'm assuming Sally contacted you either late Sunday evening, or early Monday morning. She must have been concerned when Claire didn't arrive as planned?'

Tomlinson shuffled in the chair, looked away. After half a minute, he returned his gaze to Watts. 'The thing is, Detective Watts, Sally doesn't have either our landline, or my mobile number. I suppose she must have assumed something cropped up. That Claire, for whatever reason, couldn't make it.'

'Still, why didn't *you* contact us earlier, Mr Tomlinson?'

'Sergeant Watts, it's entirely conceivable Claire lied about where she was going. Either that, or she changed her mind at the last minute. I don't know. I'm not my wife's keeper!'

Watts's brow furrowed. 'Lied? Changed her mind? Sorry, Mr Tomlinson, I'm not with you.'

'What I'm saying is... Claire could have been economical with the truth.'

Watts failed to conceal his surprise. 'Why would you think that, Mr Tomlinson? Why would your wife be *economical* with the truth?'

Tomlinson sniffed, averted his eyes, glowered. 'Because she was having a bloody affair, that's why.'

'I see. I'm sorry.'

'Of course, I've known for some time she's been seeing someone. I'm just... You know... Thinking things through. Considering my options. I thought we understood one another. Now, I'm not so sure. Since there's a child involved, Detective Watts, it's a delicate situation.'

'I can only imagine.'

'You don't have children?'

'No,' Watts said, pausing. 'Mr Tomlinson, I'm sorry to have to ask you this... Only, is there any possibility Claire's with this other man?'

'I suppose it's possible.'

'Then why, sir, are you worried she hasn't come home? I'm sure an educated man like you, appreciates wasting police time is a very serious matter.'

Tomlinson glared. 'Because of our daughter, Detective Watts, that's why.' Tomlinson sucked a long breath. 'Emily had a ballet class diarised at five this afternoon. Claire would never let Emily down. It's obvious, despite what she says to the contrary, Claire doesn't give a flying fig about our marriage, but she'd walk through fire before letting Emily down.'

'I see.'

Watts pondered where to take the conversation next.

'So, let me get this straight. Your wife, Claire, left home at six o'clock on Sunday evening. Since then, you've had no contact with her – no phone calls, texts, emails, nothing? Is that correct?'

A nod. 'Correct. I've tried her phone hundreds of times, but all I keep getting is the dead tone. It's not even going to voicemail. Doesn't that strike you as odd, Detective Watts?'

'Yes, it does. I take it your wife hasn't contacted your daughter, Emily?'

'The answer to your question is, no. She hasn't contacted Emily direct. Which, I might add, is totally out of character,' said Tomlinson, drawing breath. 'Look, Sergeant Watts, I'm going to level with you. I've just experienced the worst weekend of my life. I've grave concerns for my wife's welfare. Christ knows where she's got to. The thing is...'

'Go on.'

'There's something I'd like to get off my chest.'

'OK.'

'Before I do... Any chance of a hot drink? I'm spitting feathers.'

'Of course. I'm sorry, I should have offered you one,' said Watts, rising. 'What would you like? A tea? Coffee?'

'Coffee, please. Black. And strong.'

'I won't be a minute,' said Watts.

CHAPTER TWO

TUESDAY 1ST AUGUST, **9.15 p.m.**

'It all kicked off, Saturday morning. Emily had gone into town with her pals. Claire and I were alone in the house. I'd just taken a call from a good friend of mine.'

'Before you continue, this friend of yours, Mr Tomlinson, their name?'

'Charles Knight. Charlie's one of the founding partners of the company I part own. When Charlie retired, I bought his shares. That was in 2012. Charlie's a lifelong friend of my father.'

Watts raised a hand. 'Sorry to interrupt, again, I need to get this down,' said Watts, scribbling furiously. 'Please, continue.'

'As I was saying, Charlie's been a family friend for as long as I can remember. I took a call from him on Saturday morning. It had just gone ten. I could tell something was bothering him. He told me he'd just put the phone down to a mutual acquaintance. A chap I vaguely know called Andy Mell. Myself and Claire sat next to Mell at one of those black tie charity auctions last Christmas. Seems Mell was drinking in his local, The Rose and Crown in Osmotherley, on Friday night. He was propping up the bar, like you do, when he recognised Claire sat in a booth with a local man that he knew – a flash bastard called Owen Boyd. Boyd is a ladies' man. Tosser drives an Aston, owns a speedboat on Lake Windermere. I'm sure you know the type. Charlie tells me he's a financial adviser for some huge American corporation, working out of their Leeds office. Anyway, as the night progressed, Claire and Boyd became increasingly voluble. They argued. The landlord asked them to leave, and they had a slanging match in the car park. I'm told it got heated. Boyd took off. But not before he'd kicked over several planters, overturned a couple of benches and dragged the wing mirror off of the landlord's Jag.'

'And this mutual acquaintance, this Andy Mell, he's sure it was your wife, Claire, with Boyd?'

'Detective Watts, Mell sat between myself and Claire for the best part of four hours at the charity do. Mell told Charlie it amazed him that Claire never recognised him. I suppose she must have been well on her way. Claire can devour a bottle of Prosecco faster than you can say pissed-up yummy mummy.'

Watts tried hard not to smirk. 'OK. What did you do next? How did you feel?'

'How do you think I bloody felt? Devastated. Angry. Hurt. Most of all, furious. When I took the call from Charlie, Claire was upstairs, asleep in bed. Before I'd come downstairs, she'd mumbled something about having a thick head. After I'd spoken to Charlie, I went for a drive to clear *my* head. I didn't want to create a scene. I mean, there was Emily to consider. She, too, was upstairs in bed, asleep.'

'Where did you go?'

'I drove to a quiet spot I know along the River Tees, sat on a log and watched the river go by. I watched the kingfishers and dippers. Amazing bird the Kingfisher: fair glows in the sunlight. I go there often to think. I used fish that stretch of the river with my father when I was a boy. I must have spent two hours there, alone, contemplating what to do for the best. When I switched on my mobile, Claire had left several messages, wondering where I was. I called her back. Decided it would be better if we talked when there was physical distance between us. As I say, I couldn't see any point in creating a scene, with emotions running high. I've never been one to let my emotions get the better of me.'

'Sorry to ask you this, Mr Tomlinson. Did your wife admit to having an affair with Boyd when you told her about the phone call from Mr Knight? I'm a little confused.'

'If truth be known, I already knew she was having an affair before Charlie's phone call.'

'You did?'

'Yes, because Claire walked out on me last Wednesday evening. She came home for some stuff on Thursday evening. I talked her round. She cried. Said the affair was a drunken fling that had got out of hand. She said she loved me. Said she'd do anything to save the marriage. Begged me for forgiveness. Told me it would never happen again.' Tomlinson drew breath, shook his head. 'It might seem strange, Detective Watts, but we agreed she would see Boyd one last time and end the relationship with him on Friday night. I didn't want there to be any ambiguity on his part. She said she'd tried to end it, the affair, but he wasn't having it. He was pissed off because he'd given up everything to be with Claire. Left his fiancée and moved into a flat he owns in Osmotherley. Smarmy bastard wanted Claire to move in with him. My head was spinning. I told Claire I needed time. Time to think things through. I didn't expect them to get drunk and end up having a slanging match in full public view. So, Saturday afternoon, I packed an overnight back and took myself off. I drove to a B&B in Helmsley. It's a place we use when we go hiking in the Dales. I booked in for one night – Saturday night.'

Watts interjected: 'Did you speak to your wife while you were at the B&B?'

'No. Most of Saturday, Claire kept badgering me with text messages asking for forgiveness. I asked her to stop. I needed time to get my head around the situation. After a while, she got the message. The texts stopped. I arrived home just before midday on Sunday. I dropped Emily off at a friend's house for Sunday lunch around one o'clock. When I got back, Claire and I talked. We agreed we'd try again, not only for Emily's sake, but for the sake of our marriage, too. I hated... No, *hate*, what she did, but I'm not one to bear a grudge. On Sunday afternoon we ended up in bed together. It was tender. Just like we were newlyweds again.'

'I see. And was Claire's visit to Masham pre-arranged?'

'Yes, it's been on the calendar for months. One of Sally's regular girls was off on holiday to the Canaries, and Sally needed an extra pair of hands. Claire hates to let people down. We agreed some space would be a good thing. Claire hates to let people down. We kissed and cuddled on the doorstep.' Tomlinson stalled. 'I only hope there's a simple explanation for all of this. You don't think she's come to any harm, do you, Sergeant Watts?'

David Watts shook his head. 'I'm sure your wife is perfectly safe,' said Watts, whilst thinking precisely the opposite.

CHAPTER THREE

WEDNESDAY 2ND AUGUST, **11:00 a.m.**

Ellie Marshall – sister of Claire Tomlinson – sat across the table from Detective Inspector Alan Wardell. The interview room was five square metres of cheap furniture and nondescript decor. The none-too-subtle aroma of furniture polish thick in the air.

'How can I help, Mrs Marshall?'

'Thank you for seeing me, Inspector. I'm here about my sister, Claire Tomlinson. I'm worried about her.'

'I see. Any reason for that?'

'Yes. Claire was staying over Sunday night until Tuesday afternoon. She never arrived. It's not like her. I spoke Claire's husband, Drew, late Monday afternoon. He purported not to know where she was. To be honest, Inspector, I don't think he gives a damn.'

'Really?'

'Yes, really. I tried contacting Drew late Sunday night on his mobile, but he wasn't picking up. He dodged my calls most of

Monday. When I caught up with him late Monday afternoon, he was very brusque. He told me to "keep my effing nose out". I suspect he was drunk. Idiot put the phone down on me.'

'He did, did he?'

'Yes, he did. To tell you the truth, Inspector, we've never hit it off. Drew's always been stand-offish and, more often than not, downright rude, with Tim and I.'

'Tim?'

'My husband.'

'Any reason, why?'

'Before Tim took voluntary redundancy, he managed the local branch of Barclays. In 2009, Tim and Drew had a run-in. It concerned the overdue repayment of a business loan. It was during the recession, and Drew's company was haemorrhaging money. Drew took umbrage. He ended up closing the business account and taking the company's business elsewhere.' Ellie Marshall looked to her hands, bothered at a ragged cuticle. Returned her gaze to Wardell. 'It was all rather unseemly. As you might imagine, it did nothing for family harmony. Anyway, I've not come here to discuss Drew bloody Tomlinson. I'm here about Claire. She's the one I care about.'

'When did you last speak with your sister, Mrs Marshall?'

'Last Sunday, around teatime, on the phone. She sounded upset. She had made plans to help her friend Sally out in her tearoom in Masham. Told me she was going to call Sally and cry off. She said she couldn't face putting on a brave face to the public.'

'What time was this? It may be important.'

'About quarter past six. She said she was parked in a lay-by on the road between Thimbleby – where she lives – and Osmotherley.'

'How long did the call last?'

'Ten minutes.'

'Did you discuss anything else?'

'That's the thing, Inspector, she was being melodramatic. She confided in me she's been having an affair for the past two months. She told me she'd left home on Wednesday evening and returned on Thursday teatime to collect bits and pieces. That's when they – Claire and Drew – had a blazing row. He'd talked her out of leaving, but not before the police had called round about the noise. Emily had panicked and dialled 999.' Ellie drew breath. 'Sorry, Inspector, I suffer from anxiety.'

'That's all right, take your time. There's no hurry.'

'Thank you. It's one of the many crosses I have to bear. Anyway, Claire had agreed with Drew that she would see this guy – this boyfriend – on Friday night, to make sure he understood the affair was over. They met up in a pub in Osmotherley. When Claire told him she was ending the relationship, he went berserk. There was a scene. The landlord asked them to leave. That's when he – the boyfriend – flipped. Things got knocked around. Through a friend of a friend, Drew got wind of the altercation in the pub on Saturday morning. Someone recognised Claire. Drew was furious. He stormed out. But not before he'd threatened to kill, Claire.' Ellie Marshall sucked a long breath. 'Drew had booked himself into a B&B in Helmsley on Saturday night. He told Claire he needed time on his own to get his head around what had happened. She told me they'd had several long and emotional telephone conversations on Saturday night. By the end of the day, they'd agreed to give it another go. It, being their marriage.'

'Did Claire say anything about the boyfriend? Whether she had spoken to him after the argument on Friday night?'

'Yes, she did. That's why I'm so worried, Inspector. She told me she was meeting up with him at his flat to collect her things before coming over to my place. I expected her to arrive no later than nine o'clock on Sunday night. That's the last thing Claire said. Inspector, I know my sister better than anyone. I'm not convinced her heart was into a reconciliation with Drew.'

'You weren't?'

'No, I wasn't. I can tell when Claire's holding out on me. Tell when she's being coy, hedging her bets.'

'You believed she was?'

'I did, yes. Claire's never been a good liar. I could tell from the tone of her voice that she wasn't one hundred percent sure of her own mind. Of course, I kept my counsel. She's an adult. She can make her own bed, and she can most certainly lie in it.'

'This boyfriend, did Claire mention his name?'

'I'm afraid she didn't, no. Sorry.'

'So, why come to us now?'

'At quarter to eleven on Sunday night, I received this text message from Claire's mobile. I'd sent her a text at ten o'clock asking her what was delaying her.'

Ellie Marshall passed Wardell her mobile phone. Wardell studied the text. Noted the time.

THANKS FOR LISTENING. FOR BEING THERE. I'M RETHINKING THINGS. I'LL BE LATE. PROBABLY PAST MIDNIGHT. IF I COME... I'LL LET MYSELF IN. CHANCE I MIGHT NOT MAKE IT. SORRY FOR MESSING YOU AROUND. LOVE YOU, C xxx

'Claire's got a house key. I knew then that she had changed her mind about making up with Drew. I don't blame her. Drew is a knob. Scrub that. He's an arrogant bastard. I sent Claire several text messages on Monday and several more yesterday, without reply. I've tried ringing, but all I keep getting is the dead tone. Her phone isn't even going to voicemail. It's not like her, Inspector. You don't think something bad has happened to her, do you? As I say, I'm worried.'

'I hope not,' said Wardell, without hesitation. 'Mrs Marshall, can I take your contact details? It's a sad fact, many hundreds of people go missing in the UK every week. The good news is, most turn up unharmed within days.' Keen to end the meeting, Wardell stood and collected his things. 'We'll circulate Claire's details and make the National Missing Persons Unit aware. In the meantime, we'll start making enquiries. Please, try not to worry, Mrs Marshall. I'm sure your sister is safe and well. I expect she needs a little time on her own.'

'I hope you're right, Inspector. I'm letting my imagination run away with itself. Will you promise to keep me informed?'

'I will. You did the right thing coming in, Mrs Marshall. If Claire turns up, or contacts you, let us know. OK?'

'I will,' said Ellie Marshall, pocketing her mobile phone.

CHAPTER FOUR

WEDNESDAY 2ND AUGUST, **2:00 p.m.**

Wardell waved at Watts over the partition between their desks. 'Pull up a chair, David. I need to bend your ear.'

Watts, rolling around the partition in his chair, crashed to a halt against Wardell.

'Sorry, guv. Bloody momentum caught me out. What's up?'

'Claire Tomlinson.'

'Who?'

'The missing woman from Thimbleby. Her sister, Ellie, came in earlier; husband, Drew, last night. You took a statement. Ring any bells, yet?'

'Oh, yeah, those two. Sorry, I'm with you now. I've slept since.'

'Two things. First, we'll interview the fancy man, Boyd. Second, we need to speak to the husband again. The longer Claire Tomlinson's missing, the more concerned I am. Something doesn't smell right, David.' Wardell scratched his chin. 'Claire

Tomlinson goes missing after coming clean about having an affair on the Thursday. The following night, she's arguing with the fancy man in the pub. Then, less than forty-eight hours later, she goes missing. Concerning.'

'Anything specific bugging you, guv?'

'Lots of things, David.'

'Go on.'

'Drew Tomlinson forgot to mention that uniform attended a domestic at his home on the Thursday evening of last week.'

'The Thursday before she went AWOL on Sunday?' asked Watts.

'That's right. The daughter, Emily, dialled 999 and told the operator that Daddy was scaring her. She said Daddy had gone mad. Was throwing things around. Yelling about hurting, Mummy.'

'I agree it was remiss of him, not to mention it,' Watts said. 'He must have been ashamed, I suppose.'

'Maybe. I've spoken to uniform. They told me that by the time they'd arrived, things had calmed down. Claire said it was nothing. She laughed it off. Said Emily had panicked. And there was nothing to worry about.'

'OK.'

'According to Tomlinson, she would never let Emily down. Also, the wording of her text message to her sister on Sunday night suggests she'd keep her sister informed of her movements. They seem close. Most worrying of all, according to Ellie Marshall, Drew threatened to kill Claire in a heated argument on Saturday morning.'

'I see what you're getting at. OK. What do you want me to do?'

'Get on the blower. Speak to Owen Boyd. Say we'll meet him at his apartment in Osmotherley. I'd like to see this particular lothario in his natural environment. Before we do, we'll drop in at

The Rose and Crown. See if we can't speak to someone who witnessed this argument between Claire Tomlinson and Owen Boyd, on Friday night.'

'Sounds like a plan, guv. I could murder a swift half. And the husband?'

'I'll brief Bina. Get her to talk to him.'

CHAPTER FIVE

Wardell and Watts entered The Rose and Crown, ambled over to the bar and ordered two halves. They introduced themselves to the twenty-something barmaid – a stick-thin, gaunt-faced girl, in skinny jeans and a Nirvana T-shirt, with coal-black hair tied in a ponytail. Within a minute, Wardell had established she had worked the Friday night shift.

'Do you know Owen Boyd?'

'Course I do. Owen's a regular here. Comes in most Friday and Saturday nights. Anyone who's anyone in Osmotherley knows Owen. Owen thinks of himself as the big shot around here. He's the type that loves to splash the cash. People gravitate to his type, don't they?'

Wardell shrugged. 'I suppose they do. A little bird told me he came in Friday night. Is that right?'

'Yeah, that's right. Your little bird, he or she, knows a thing or two. He came in with a blonde I've never seen before. Snotty cow, she was.'

'Why do you say that?'

'Because she went off on one when I told her we'd run out of slimline tonic, that's why. She was downing G&Ts like it was going out of fashion. She stormed off. I mean, what's it got to do with me? I was only doing my sodding job. I don't do the ordering.'

'I see.' Wardell paused. 'So, tell me... What else do you remember about Friday night? Was Owen Boyd on his best behaviour?'

An eyes wide look of surprise. 'Hardly. The pair of 'em came in about eight o'clock. They sat in a booth by the window. For the first hour, they shared a bottle of champagne. Lanson, it was. Pricey. After that, they started on the G&Ts and lager. As the night progressed, they got louder and louder. I could see Jim – he's the landlord here – was getting annoyed. He gave them the Scarborough warning. Asked them to keep it down.'

'What time approximately?'

'About quarter past ten. Yeah, that would be about right, quarter past ten. The kitchen staff had just left. They finish at ten. They don't hang around once they've cleaned up.'

'Did Boyd and the blonde quieten down after the landlord spoke to them?'

'For a while they did, yeah.'

'What do you mean, for a while?'

'About half an hour later, things got heated. They swapped insults. Created a scene.'

'In what way?'

'I overheard him call her a backstabber. He said she'd led him up the garden path. That he'd make her pay. Said he'd left his fiancée for nothing. He was going mental. It was entertaining.

Just like something out of Eastenders. Most nights, it's like a sodding morgue in here. Usually, I'm bored out of my brain.'

'And she sat there and let him insult her?'

'Did she hell as like. She jumped up and chucked his pint over him. Fortunately for him, there was only half a pint left. The look on his face was priceless. You could hear a pin drop. That's when Jim asked them to leave. Owen called Jim a knobhead. Jim grabbed him by the scruff, dragged him to the door, gave him a kick up the arse and threw him out.'

'What happened next?'

'Once they were outside, that's when it kicked off. Owen grabbed her by the wrist and tried for a kiss. She pushed him away, and he fell arse over tit over a bench and cracked his head on the pavement. It was hilarious. Owen went crazy. He smashed up four of the six benches and kicked over all the planters. Jim rushed outside and made the woman come inside, for her own safety as much as anything. Once inside, he threw the locks. We'd been watching with our noses pressed up against the window. Jim went round to Boyd's flat first thing Saturday morning and posted a letter demanding he pay a grand in compensation. He threatened Boyd that he'd get you lot involved if he didn't stump up the readies. Owen dropped off an envelope containing the money on Monday evening. Rich git. As you might expect, he's barred now.'

'What happened to the woman – the blonde?'

'Once everything had calmed down, we called a taxi to take her home.'

'What time was this?'

'It was just after midnight when she left. I've not seen her since. Before she left, we made her drink several cups of strong, black coffee. She was in a right state. She had a shocking bruise on her forearm. Once she'd sobered up, to be fair, she seemed like a nice lady. I felt sorry for her. She's not come to any harm, has she?'

'Not as far as we know,' said Wardell, downing the last dregs of ale. 'Thank you for your time.'

'No problem. Anytime. If you do see Owen, tell him not to bother darkening Jim's door again. Unless, that is, he wants another kick up the arse.'

Wardell chuckled. Turned. And set off for the door.

CHAPTER SIX

'Mr Boyd? Mr Owen Boyd?'

'Yes, that's right. Who's asking?'

Boyd's wide eyes flitted to Wardell and Watts. His demeanour changed, became tense, like a cornered rodent under the gaze of a rearing cobra. In unison, the detectives showed their warrant cards.

'I'm Detective Inspector Alan Wardell. This is my colleague, Detective Sergeant David Watts. We're with North Yorkshire Police Major Crime Unit. David spoke to you on the phone.'

'OK. Impressive. What's this about?'

'Can we come in? I don't like to discuss sensitive matters on doorsteps.'

Boyd shrugged, moved aside to allow the advancing cobras passage. Gestured, with a roll of the hand. 'If you must. We'll talk in the kitchen. The lounge's in a state. I had colleagues around last night. I haven't got round to clearing up, yet. Follow me.'

Seated around the kitchen table, Boyd studied Wardell and Watts with suspicious hollow eyes, underslung by dark circles.

'Go ahead, gentlemen. I'm all ears.'

Wardell cleared his throat. Watts sat with a pencil poised over a fresh notebook page.

'Mr Boyd, I understand you've been having in a relationship with a married woman – a certain Mrs Claire Tomlinson. Is there any truth in it?'

A sickly grin settled on Boyd's lean face. His grin morphed to a frown. 'And what if I have been? I'm no criminal lawyer, however, I'm fairly certain seeing a married woman behind her husband's back, is, as yet, not an actual crime. Anyone who thinks it is, ought to get a bloody life. Do you agree, Inspector?'

'You're entitled to your opinion, sir. It's not for me to judge. My job is to apply the law, not make it, or make moral judgements.'

'Good. I'm delighted to hear it. In answer to your question, yes, I was seeing Claire. What do you want to know?'

'For your information, sir, no one has seen or heard from Claire Tomlinson since six o'clock Sunday evening. When did you last see, or contact, Claire Tomlinson?'

'The Friday night just gone,' said Boyd, without hesitation, shrugging, his expression souring.

'Where was this, sir?'

'We had a bust up at my local, The Rose and Crown. But I expect you already know that.'

'Why would we, sir?'

'Because, Inspector, Osmotherley is a small place. Tongues have a nasty habit of wagging. Everyone knows everyone else's bloody business.'

'This bust up,' Wardell paused, 'what was it about?'

Boyd seemed unsure of himself.

'Before I tell you what happened, perhaps a little background information would be useful. It might help to put the events of Friday night into context. That night will forever haunt me.'

'OK, sir. When you're ready.'

'Claire and I first met at the gym about a year ago. We were sitting in the jacuzzi and we got talking, like you do. We hit it off. As fate would have it, we kept bumping into one another. About two months ago, I bumped into her in town. It was late on a Thursday afternoon. My fiancée, Teresa, was away on a course in London. She's a business development manager with a cosmetics company and she works away from home a lot. Anyway, I asked Claire if she'd like a drink. We drank several glasses of wine in a bistro. One thing led to another. And we ended up back at my place. I'm sure you can guess the rest. Of course, I felt guilty as hell going behind Teresa's back like that. Without going into detail, Claire is special. She's a one in a million. We started meeting up once a week in the afternoons. We'd drive to a secluded place I know a couple of miles north of here. It's a lovely spot called Devil's Bridge. Awful name. Beautiful place. The sex was fantastic. Not wishing to brag, gentlemen, since I've had my fair share, I like to think I know the difference. Our relationship was never just about the sex. I loved, love, Claire. She told me she felt the same about me. And do you know something, gentlemen, like a mug, I believed her. She agreed to leave her husband. We made plans. The tenancy here was up for renewal. I own three identical one bed apartments in this block. They're my pension pot. Are you keeping up, gentlemen?'

'Yes. When did you move in, Mr Boyd?'

'A month ago. Mid-July. By now, Claire ought've moved in, too.'

'I take it she got cold feet?'

'You could say that, yes. Overnight, last Thursday to be exact, don't ask me why because I haven't got a bloody clue, Claire Tomlinson became the ice lady. Let me explain.'

'Please.'

'Last Wednesday, Claire walked out on Drew. He's a controlling bastard. She told him she was leaving him and spent the night here with me. On Thursday, she went home to collect some bits and pieces. I reckon that's when the enormity of leaving home dawned on her. The thing is, Claire has a teenage daughter to consider. There was a massive argument and a baring of souls. Somehow – don't ask me how – Drew planted seeds of doubt in her mind. When I met up with her on Friday night, she was a changed woman. For the first couple of hours, she was all sweetness and light. It didn't last. Any idiot could see she had something on her mind. As the night progressed, I might as well have been talking to an empty shell, like no one was home. I admit I got annoyed. She'd closed down. Towards the end of the night, she told me it was over. It, being me and her. She said we could never be together. I'm ashamed to say the drink got the better of me. We argued. We exchanged insults. I can't remember what I said, but the next thing I knew, Claire had thrown a pint over me. I flipped. Anyone would. The landlord, Jim, threw me out by the scruff. Once outside, I'm ashamed to say, I lost it big style. I have a vague recollection of overturning benches, kicking planters over and glass being smashed. Doing all that cost me a grand. I felt she'd led me up the garden path. I'd left Teresa on a promise, only to get dumped like I was a spotty teenager at the disco. Christ knows when I'll be able to show my face again in The Rose and Crown. In summary, the last time I saw Claire was around eleven o'clock Friday night, as Jim marched her back into the pub. He locked the door behind him. I took the sensible option – buggered off and got myself a kebab. Ruined my best shirt, I did. Got chilli sauce all down it.'

'Have you had any contact with Claire Tomlinson since?'

'None. It's as though I've fallen off the end of the world. Look, I admit I've tried contacting her, but all I keep getting is a strange dead tone. I expect she's switched off her mobile, or barred me, or something. Has she?'

'I've no idea, sir. We'll check with her service provider. What would you say to Mrs Tomlinson if you were able to speak to her?'

'First, I'd apologise. Then...' Boyd stalled.

'Yes?'

'Then, I'd try for a reconciliation. As I say, Claire is special. She's worth fighting for.'

CHAPTER SEVEN

SATURDAY 5TH AUGUST, **2:00 p.m.**

Watts drove the unmarked Mondeo past the entrance to the caravan park and braked to a halt at the *POLICE DO NOT CROSS* tape. Grinning, he dropped the window, winked and held up his warrant card at the WPC. The young officer inspected the card, nodded, stepped around the bonnet and lowered the tape. Watts – face frozen in a grin – drove a mile along the secluded lane, bordered by high moorland and tall pines to the gravel car park at Devil's Bridge.

Wardell turned to Watts. 'Nice secure cordon, David. Give my compliments to uniform.'

'Yes, guv,' said Watts, casting a glance at the throng of journalists waiting impatiently behind the cordon and receding in the rear-view mirror. 'I wonder who tipped the press off?'

'Jungle drums, I expect,' said Wardell. 'My money is on someone from the caravan park. Is Kenny G gracing us with his presence?'

'Yes, guv. Bina texted me. He arrived an hour ago. She's nipped off to use the little girl's room at the caravan park. No doubt, he'll be in a mood.'

'Why?'

'Uniform dragged him off the tenth at Alwoodley. He was three under par.'

A hint of a grin from Wardell. 'Ugh, serves the flash bugger right. Lifestyles of the rich and bloody famous. I was glad of the call. I was sodding weeding. My back's broken.' With pain twisting his face into a grimace, Wardell massaged his right hip. 'Don't worry about, Kenny, he'll survive. And Ms Phelan? Is she expected?'

A nod and a boyish smirk from Watts. 'Yes, guv, within the hour. I'm amazed how committed she is. Not often do pathologists attend crime scenes, do they, guv?'

'No, they don't.'

Watts pulled up alongside a CSI van, parked beside a crime scene tent, shielding the locus from prying eyes.

'Better get suited and booted. We wouldn't want to compromise evidence and incur the wrath of Goddard, now would we?'

'No, sir, we would not.'

* * *

'Knock, knock,' Wardell said, peeping in through the plastic flap. 'Can we come in?'

'Alan. David. Nice to see you. Don't stand there on ceremony, gentlemen, come in. Join the party,' said Goddard, returning his gaze to the female corpse face down on the edge of a grey and black-flecked wool rug at his feet. 'Just don't touch a thing.'

Wardell entered and stood with his back pressed against the

tent wall. He peered past Goddard's left shoulder. 'We know the form, Kenny.'

'I'm very glad to hear it. Would you like my amateur hypothesis on how this young lady met her rather unfortunate demise? I'm afraid it's rather more complex than it would first appear.'

'Shoot,' said Wardell.

'Oh, she hasn't been shot, Alan.'

'Ha – bloody – ha. You know what I mean. Pray tell your conclusions, young Sherlock,' said Wardell, with a wry grin.

'I'm only joshing. OK. Let's get down to business. First things first. As you know, I'm a Scene of Crime Officer, not a pathologist. I understand Miss Phelan is on her way here as we speak. This is for your ears, only. What follows is a best guess – *my* best guess. As usual, the formal forensic report will follow in due course. Happy?'

'Delirious,' returned Wardell. 'Get on with it, Kenny. We won't hold you to anything.'

'Righto,' said Goddard, lowering onto his haunches alongside the victim's head, running a finger vertically through the air an inch above the rancid wound. 'She's been dead for some time. Best guess, about a week. Young lady suffered significant blunt force trauma injury to the back of the head. The weapon used was of circular in section, an inch in diameter and metallic. Her skull is most likely fractured in multiple places. The blow itself would not have resulted in death. It most certainly would have incapacitated her, though. She would have lost consciousness. Whilst unconscious, there's evidence to suggest someone drowned her in the beck, removed her from the water, and placed the body under the pines. Once there, they wrapped the body in a rug and piled stones over it. In what, on the face of it, appears to be a rather amateurish attempt at concealment.'

'On the ball as usual, Kenny. Drowned, eh? How did you come to that conclusion?'

'The bluish tinge to her lips. However, it's not conclusive evidence of death by drowning. Of more significance, we recovered aquatic vegetation and pebbles from the victim's clenched right fist. Pebbles are found in running water. It shows she was alive while submerged. I'm confident Ms Phelan will find waterborne, microscopic algae in her mouth, trachea and lungs.'

'Murdered then?'

Goddard nodded. 'She was, Alan.'

'Confidence level.'

'One hundred percent.'

'Clothes? Identification? Phone?'

'At the moment, none of the above, I'm afraid. I'm expecting the rug will yield all manner of forensic gems. Establishing where it originated will be the hard part.'

Wardell ran a hand over his chin. 'We'll conduct a thorough search of the immediate vicinity. Establish if the killer dumped anything hereabouts,' said Wardell.

'Any evidence of sexual assault, Mr Goddard?' asked Watts.

'Please, call me Kenny, David. Not as you'd notice, no. That said, there's minor bruising around the vulva and entrance to the vagina. I don't consider it as anything untoward. The good news is, we've recovered a viable semen sample from the cervix. Within ten hours before death, she'd had sex.'

'Excellent. Is that all?' asked Wardell.

'That's all for now, yes. Guesswork I can come up with quickly. Scientifically based, definitive forensic evidence that will stand up in a court of law, takes a little longer.'

'That's brilliant, Kenny. Get a shifty on and you'll be able to finish your round. I'm told they dragged you off the golf course. That right?'

'They did. Not a chance. She who must be obeyed is dragging me out to a book club do. I've got to get home, get my hair washed, nails done and my glad rags on. We're supposed to be there by eight.'

A smirking Wardell turned to Watts. 'Just like I told you, David, lifestyles of the rich and famous.'

Goddard rolled his eyes, turned away. 'I must get back to work. Goodbye, gentlemen. Best of luck finding the killer. And don't you dare hesitate to give me a bell should you need to.'

CHAPTER EIGHT

MONDAY 7TH AUGUST, **11:00 a.m**

DS David Watts's brain pulsed with the mother and father of headaches. A year previously – still hurting from marital break-down – agreeing to tag along on a friend-of-a-friend's stag weekend in Amsterdam had seemed like a good idea. Now, he wasn't so sure. His guts churned. A dozen Dutch maidens in clogs danced a raucous ceilidh inside his head. He ran a furry tongue around a rank-tasting mouth.

Watts drove the Mondeo into a free space by the mortuary entrance and killed the engine. Settling his head against the head-rest, he exhaled a long, exaggerated sigh.

Wardell tutted. 'You sure you're OK?' asked Wardell from the passenger seat. 'Silly sod, you ought to have phoned in sick. You stink like a brewery. And you've barely said a word all morning.'

Wardell sprung the door, stepped out of the car and leaned into the cabin.

'Sit this one out. I don't want you chucking up and making a bloody spectacle of yourself. There's a café a mile up the road. Go get yourself something to eat. And coffee. Strong. It'll do you good. Pick me up in half an hour. Won't take any longer than that. OK?'

Watts smiled a weary smile, gave a weak thumbs up, removed his hands from the door handle and set the key in the ignition. 'Thanks, guv. I feel shocking. I owe you one.'

'Yeah, whatever,' said Wardell, slamming the door and striding off, making a note to himself to blot Watts's copybook.

* * *

Wardell knocked on the postmortem room door and stepped back. As he waited, he ran olbas oil under his nostrils and hoped never to grow accustomed to the heady and unpleasant stench of death.

'Enter,' boomed a female voice from inside the room.

Wardell entered a bright, sterile canvas of white ceramic wall tiling, spotless green linoleum flooring and polished stainless-steel appliances. The naked corpse of a blonde female lay on an examination table in the centre of the room. A neatly stitched Y-shaped incision ran from the top of the woman's pubic hair to the sternum, and diagonally to both shoulders. A sickly sweet, cheesy tang heavy in the air.

Forensic pathologist Amanda Phelan stood over a Belfast sink soaping her hands and forearms. Glancing left, she smiled at Wardell.

'Morning, Alan,' Phelan said. 'Fancy a brew? This forensic pathology malarkey is thirsty work.'

'I don't mind if I do, thanks,' said Wardell.

Phelan flicked the kettle on with her right elbow, said: 'Come alone?'

'Yes. And no.'

'Sorry? I'm not with you.'

'David dropped me off. Poor lamb's hungover. He's just got back from a three-night bender in Amsterdam. He ought to have phoned in sick. I ordered him to go get something to eat. Ever since his marriage went down the pan, he's been acting like a moody teenager. Sad so-and-so.'

'I see. I suppose you can't blame him,' said Phelan, adding instant coffee to mugs, adding milk. 'Relationship breakup is a killer.'

'I suppose...' said Wardell, half-heartedly.

Wardell turned to the examination table.

'All done and dusted, I see.'

'I am. And very informative it was, too.'

Phelan handed Wardell a steaming mug.

'Here you go, Alan. Careful. It's boiling.'

Wardell accepted the mug. 'Thank you.'

'You're welcome.'

A frisson of warmth, of something more, passed between them. They stepped over to the examination table, clutching mugs.

Looking down, Phelan cleared her throat. 'Would you prefer the abbreviated version?'

'If you wouldn't mind. I've got a million and one things on my plate.'

'Victim is Mrs Claire Tomlinson, 34, married, from Thimbleby, near Osmotherley. Husband, Drew, and dental records, confirmed her identity. She was murdered. Incapacitated by a single blow to the skull and drowned. Indications are, the murder weapon was a circular steel bar, measuring a smidgeon over an inch in diameter. A wheel brace being the most likely suspect. She's been dead one week, or thereabouts.'

'You can be that specific about the murder weapon?'

'Yes, I can. I examined a near identical wound on another murder victim, a couple of months ago. That said, as I've just mentioned, the actual cause of death was drowning.'

'You're sure about that?'

'Yes. There's evidence of froth in her airways, and indications of cerebral oedema. Water was present in her stomach and lungs. Drowning is never clean cut. Lots of things to consider. With my amateur sleuth head on, I reckon the assailant surprised her from behind, struck her with a wheel brace and while she was semi-conscious, dragged her into the beck. Indications are, he held her face down, underwater, until she stopped breathing. There's evidence of pressure being applied between her shoulder blades with a size nine. Sadly, no viable footprint was recovered, which is a shame.'

Wardell frowned, ran a fingertip's worth of olbas oil deep into his nostrils, and said: 'Kenny G recovered pebbles and trace vegetation from the palms of her clenched right fist. He thinks – likely as not – they're from the bottom of the beck, which is entirely consistent with what you're saying. He mentioned the possibility of microscopic algae in her mouth, throat and lungs. Did you find any?'

'I did. Seems we've come to the same conclusion.'

'It would seem so, yes.'

'Another thing, Alan. See those cuts and abrasions across her breasts and shoulders?'

Wardell leaned in, eyes narrowing, pinching his nostrils together. 'The rash?'

'Yes. I reckon contact with the riverbed caused it.'

Wardell slurped coffee, said: 'Seems to me someone subjected her to a frenzied, blitz-type attack from behind, then drowned her,' Wardell said. 'That right?'

'I would say so, yes. As she entered the water – because of the temperature differential – she would've regained consciousness, hence the pebbles and vegetation in her clenched fist. However, by then, it was too late.'

'She never stood a chance,' said Wardell.

'No, she didn't. By the way... How's the coffee?'

'Great, thanks,' returned Wardell, glancing at his wristwatch. 'Anything else?'

'Only that she'd eaten within five hours of death. I found an undigested Sunday lunch in her gut. And she'd had sex less than ten hours before she died. Whilst I don't think she was raped, the sex was rough.'

'What makes you say that?'

'She's got minor bruising around her inner thighs and vulva.'

'I see. That's not nice.'

'Yes... Well... It takes all sorts. When do you want my report?'

'There's no rush, now I've got the gist. Sorry, Amanda, but I'd better be making tracks. David will be pining. He hates being separated from his carer for too long.'

Phelan chuckled, eyes sparkling. 'I suppose you better had. Give him my regards. Tell him I hope he's feeling better soon.'

'I will. And thank you for your time. As always, it's appreciated.'

'You're welcome, Alan, anytime. Only, think on...'

'About what?'

'There's absolutely no rush to bring me any more murder victims. Every time you do, my heart breaks a little more. I'm starting to think it's beyond repair.'

'Noted,' said Wardell, turning and heading for the door.

CHAPTER NINE

'Alan. Kenny Goddard. How are you?'

'Fine, thanks. You?'

'Not bad. To tell you the truth, I'm a little miffed.'

'Why?'

'Computer system's up the spout. Damn thing has a virus. The powers that be won't let us anywhere near it. For years, I've been banging about building a secure firewall. Buggers never listen. Anyway, the reason I'm phoning, is to update you on the murder at Devil's Bridge. Something interesting has cropped up.'

'What exactly?'

'First, we've recovered fluids and a viable semen sample from the rug. Get me samples of DNA from your prime suspects, Alan, and, with a fair wind, we'll find a match. Second, we've recovered two sets of tyre tracks. Do you remember the burned-out car halfway along the lane leading to the locus?'

'I do, the Corsa.'

'That's correct. Well, across the lane from it, we found vehicle tracks in the mud. We believe – given the size and tread pattern – a 4x4 made them towing a trailer. I checked the weather records. There was a heavy rain shower in that area on Sunday evening from five till six. Before then, it was bone dry all day. Alan, those tracks were made around the time of the murder.'

'Mmm, interesting...'

'Mike spotted them and checked with the Met Office. He's razor sharp, that young man. What do you think? Any of your suspects own a 4x4, or have access to a trailer?'

'I'm not sure. To be honest, Kenny, we're still getting our heads around things. It's not the simplest of cases. I'll bear it in my as we move forward.'

'You do that. I appreciate even the smallest piece of the jigsaw can be important.'

'True enough, Kenny. Anything else?'

'Nope. I thought you'd want to know about the semen and tracks.'

'Yeah, thanks. Useful.'

'No worries. I'll email the forensic report direct to you, just as soon as the blasted computers are back online.'

CHAPTER TEN

'David. Time for a recap,' said Wardell, taking a seat opposite Watts. He stirred his tea, settled the spoon on the saucer. 'Our missing person search has become a murder investigation. The victim is Mrs Claire Tomlinson, 34, from Thimbleby, near Osmotherley, married to husband Drew for thirteen years and reported missing by him on the night of Tuesday 1st August. They have one daughter, Emily, aged 13. According to Mr Tomlinson, he last saw Claire alive as she drove away from home in Thimbleby at six o'clock on Sunday, the 30th of July. Mrs Tomlinson was at the wheel of her silver BMW 420d. The car dumped and discovered in a copse three hundred yards from the body. The killer made a half-hearted attempt at concealment. We found her mobile phone just yards from the car. Someone had switched it off. Analysis of the sim card is underway. Printouts of the call register, emails and text messages are available tomorrow morning. The killer bundled the body in a rug and built a mound of stones over it. We found the victim's clothes in undergrowth fifteen yards, from the car. According to Mr Tomlinson, they'd been home alone all of Sunday afternoon. Mr Tomlinson having dropped their daughter Emily off at a friend's house, at one. Claire told Drew she was planning to stay at her friend Sally Evans's place in Masham from Sunday night until mid-Tuesday afternoon. On her return, she was going to take Emily to her ballet lesson at five o'clock that same afternoon. Mrs Tomlinson was never seen alive again.' Wardell referred to his notes, drummed a pencil, continued: 'Mr Tomlinson reported his wife missing at 9.00 p.m., Tuesday evening. Mrs Tomlinson's sister, Ellie Marshall, came in Wednesday morning worried that Claire wasn't picking up on her mobile and hadn't stayed over as arranged on Sunday night, as discussed in their telephone conversation at 6.15 p.m. on Sunday. Claire sent a text to Ellie saying she was, "rethinking things", at quarter to eleven, Sunday night. She'd mentioned to Ellie that she was going around to Boyd's flat to pick up some of her possessions. At quarter past six, Claire phoned Ellie from a lay-by out on the Osmotherley Road. According to Ellie, after Drew had found out about the argument in the pub with Boyd on Friday night, and before he left home to stay at a B&B in Helmsley on Saturday night, Drew had threatened to kill Claire.'

'It's all a bit of a bugger's muddle, guv. I'm struggling to keep up.'

'You're not alone, David. Let's consider the suspects Drew Tomlinson and Owen Boyd. Start by considering probable motives. For the moment, we'll focus on the husband, Drew Tomlinson.'

Wardell leaned back, joined his hands behind his head and inhaled a long breath.

'When we interviewed Tomlinson, I reckon he was trying hard to portray the image of a man in total control. Someone with a cool head, who doesn't rise to the bait easily. He conveniently forgot to mention that he had threatened to kill his wife on Saturday morning, which, I suppose, is hardly surprising. He may well have said he'd kill her in the heat of the moment. Plenty do during arguments. Him, finding out that his wife of thirteen years is having an affair, and on the brink of leaving him, must've come as a shock. Let's go through it again.'

'Fine by me,' said Watts.

Wardell raised a finger after each point. 'Uniform attended Tomlinson's home address on the Thursday before the altercation with Boyd in the pub on Friday night. We now know that Drew knew about Claire's infidelity with Boyd *before* he took the phone call from a family friend, Charlie, mid-morning on Saturday. Drew might have given Claire a, '*him or me,*' ultimatum on Thursday night. Such a scenario is consistent with the barmaid overhearing Claire finishing with Boyd on Friday night. It's obvious that Boyd took it badly, lost his rag and flew into a rage.' Shifting in his seat, Wardell turned his thoughts back to the husband. 'Tomlinson claims he stayed in a B&B in Helmsley on Saturday night, ostensibly to get his head around Claire's infidelity and, if he is to be believed, to give himself thinking time. It's likely that he was still reeling about her leaving home on Wednesday.' Running out of fingers, Wardell scratched his nose, continued. 'Tomlinson stated that he and Claire had fully reconciled by early Sunday afternoon. That they had sex to consummate their renewed commitment, and the post-mortem confirmed she'd had sex in the hours before she was killed. Given the bruising, the sex was obviously of the vigorous variety, which gives a good insight into Drew Tomlinson's state of mind that day. We're yet to receive confirmation that it is Drew Tomlinson's semen. As far as Drew Tomlinson was concerned, all was well and good in the world when he alleges Claire left home on Sunday evening to travel to Masham. Despite that, he blanked his sister-in-law most of Monday. When she spoke to him late Monday afternoon, he used profanity. She's convinced he'd been drinking. Ask yourself, David, why would a professional man like Drew Tomlinson be swearing and drinking on a Monday afternoon?'

Watts joined his hands across his middle. 'I reckon Drew Tomlinson was all over the place, psychologically. From the moment Claire walked out on him on Wednesday, came home Thursday, right through to Sunday evening, he must've been experiencing a roller coaster of emotions.'

'I agree,' said Wardell. 'Perhaps he didn't think Claire was being totally honest with him about making a go of the marriage, especially when she insisted on going to Masham? Perhaps, he became suspicious and followed her. Watched her talking on the phone to Ellie in the lay-by and concluded she was talking to Boyd. Maybe he followed her to Boyd's flat. Assumed she was having a liaison with him, saw red and intercepted her en route. Either that, or intercepted her after she'd collected her possessions – which included the rug from Boyd's flat. The one she was discovered in. Then, after he'd attacked her, he drove to Devil's Bridge in her car, finished her off in the beck and disposed of the body under the stones.'

David Watts leaned in, keen to continue the hypothesis. 'That's a compelling motive if he convinced himself that she was still lying to him. Let's hope SOCO can connect the rug to Boyd's flat and Drew Tomlinson? She probably still had a key. According to Boyd, she was planning to move in.'

'That's true enough. And it would be an excellent opportunity for Tomlinson to implicate Boyd, too,' Wardell said.

'What about Boyd, guv? We know he's got a violent temper. And, in his own words, she'd led him up the garden path. He felt betrayed. Guv, some of what he said was downright creepy.'

'Creepy?'

'Yeah, creepy. All that stuff about Claire being "special".

What did he mean by it? It sent shivers down my spine. There are echoes of Hannibal Lecter there, if you ask me.'

Wardell raised his eyebrows. Not wishing to dampen Watts's enthusiasm – even though he thought Watts was being a little True Detective, he continued the thread. 'Boyd had motive. Claire had dumped him after he'd burned all his bridges with his fiancée, Teresa.' Wardell paused. 'Let's interview both men. Ask pertinent and searching questions. Get DNA samples. Sim card downloads. I'm keen to identify the producer of the semen stains found on the rug. Keen also to confirm Tomlinson is telling the truth about him having sex with Claire on Sunday afternoon. If it's confirmed that the rug is from Boyd's flat, then it's probable the semen is his. C'mon, let's get going. On the way out, pick up a couple of swab kits and your laptop.'

CHAPTER ELEVEN

WEDNESDAY 9TH AUGUST, **1:00 p.m.**

Wardell, Watts and Drew Tomlinson sat across a glass coffee table in the lounge of Tomlinson's home.

'How are you holding up, Mr Tomlinson?' said Wardell.

'How do you think I'm bloody holding up? I'm heartbroken. There's a hole in my chest where my heart used to be. I don't know which way to turn. Emily's not stopped crying since I told her some bastard murdered her mother. She's locked herself in her room and won't come out. It's a struggle to get her to eat. I'm considering asking Emily's Aunty Ellie to come round and see if she can't make her come out.'

Wardell breathed deep. Sighed. 'I'm sorry to hear that. I can't imagine how she must be feeling. Did the family liaison officer, help?'

'No. Emily's a teenager. It's a difficult age. She told the officer to piss off. There's no talking to her. We have a doctor's appointment on Friday. She's going to need time. Time to understand what's happened. Time to understand the future. Any progress identifying the killer, inspector?'

Wardell shook his head. 'It's too early to say, Mr Tomlinson. I would be lying if I told you we've come up with anything of any substance.' Wardell stalled. 'Mr Tomlinson, I know this is difficult, only... I'd like to go through the events of the week leading with you, up to your wife's disappearance. We're confused. We need to clarify what happened, when. Something insignificant, a detail, can often prove critical.'

'OK. Where would you like me to start?'

'How about Thursday evening?'

'Thursday?'

'That's right. Thursday. The night Emily dialled 999.'

'I see. I wasn't aware you knew about that.'

'Yes. Although we're low on staff, every call gets logged.'

Tomlinson shrugged. 'It was nothing. Emily's never seen us arguing. When Claire and I got married, we agreed never to argue in front of any children we might be blessed with. It was an overreaction on Emily's part, phoning the police.'

'The reason you'd been arguing, sir?'

'Because... Oh, sod it, you're going to find out, anyway.' Tomlinson said, eyes rolling. 'Lunchtime on Thursday, a third party informed me Claire was seeing someone. As I've already mentioned, she'd walked out on me, *us,* on Wednesday evening.'

'How did you find out? I want you to be clear here, Mr Tomlinson.'

'A month ago, I hired a private detective,' said Tomlinson, without preamble, expression betraying no emotion. 'Thursday lunchtime, the private detective, emailed me photos of Claire and Boyd entering Boyd's flat in Osmotherley. In one picture, the bastard was pinching Claire's arse. It turned my stomach when I saw it. There was a close-up of Claire taken through the bedroom window. She was topless. Thursday night, Claire came home to collect some things. I stuck the photos under her nose: hence the argument. We went at one another like cat and dog. It wasn't pleasant. After an hour, we burned out. That's when the boys in blue arrived. To be honest, we'd already agreed upon a ceasefire. Claire said it was a fling. Said she'd ended the relationship with Boyd. Promised, the affair had run its course. We agreed she'd meet Boyd Friday night and tell him to his face. I didn't want there was no ambiguity on his part. How was I to know Boyd would go berserk and murder Claire? Answer me that, inspector.'

Wardell's brow creased. 'We don't know that *is* the case, Mr Tomlinson.'

'What? Jesus Christ, you can't be serious! I mean, who else could have killed her? Boyd went crazy in the pub on Friday night when Claire told him she was dumping him. Witnesses saw what he did. Saturday morning she had a horrible bruise on her arm where he'd taken hold of her. It's fucking obvious that Boyd killed Claire.'

Drew Tomlinson's chin fell onto his chest and he blubbered. Tears meandered down his face and stained his shirt. Wardell and Watts exchanged wary glances. Wardell nodded towards the kitchen. Watts, taking the hint, stood and settled a hand on Drew Tomlinson's shoulder.

'Can I get you something to drink, Mr Tomlinson? A whisky or brandy, perhaps?'

Tomlinson faced Watts, dried his tears. 'Why the hell not? There's a bottle of Macallan in the utility. Make it a double. Pour one for yourself and the inspector.'

Wardell raised a hand of objection. 'Not for us. Thanks all the same.'

Watts disappeared through the door.

Wardell leaned in. Only three feet separated the two men; the fragrant peat of whisky on Tomlinson's breath, thick in the space between them.

'Mr Tomlinson, all I'm interested in, is the truth. I feel your pain. That said, I need you to describe your movements from Saturday morning, through to Monday afternoon. I'm going to need to swab inside your mouth. Forensics need to confirm it's your semen inside, Claire. Also, with your permission, I'd like to make a copy of the contents of your phone's sim card. It'll only take a minute. Sergeant Watts has a special program on his laptop.'

'Are these things absolutely necessary, inspector?'

'I'm afraid they are. Somebody took a human life. It's my job to bring that somebody to justice as soon as humanly possible.'

'I'm delighted to hear it.'

'Take your time, Mr Tomlinson.'

David Watts returned and handed Tomlinson a double whisky in a crystal tumbler. 'Your whisky.'

'Thank you.' Tomlinson sank the amber liquid in a single draught and settled the tumbler down on the table. 'Saturday night just gone, I stayed at The Willows B&B in Helmsley. You can check if you like. I woke up around half past seven on Sunday morning and enjoyed a full English. I set off for home around half-past eight. I had a good run and arrived home just before ten. Claire was upstairs, asleep in bed. Emily was asleep too. I decided not to wake Claire and nipped out for a paper. When I got back, I sat and read the paper in the conservatory. It must've been the best part of an hour before Claire came down. I made her a cuppa and toast. We sat at the kitchen table holding hands, not saying much. We do that sometimes. Claire said she'd nip upstairs and get dressed. I said why bother getting dressed? She took the hint and led me upstairs. I'm sure you can imagine the rest. With Emily across the landing, we were discreet. It turned out to be the appetiser. The main course came later that afternoon, after I'd dropped Emily off.'

Wardell nodded. Watts tried hard not to smirk.

'Afterwards, we talked. I'd never seen her so sad. Despite what she'd done, I just wanted to hold her. I told her not to worry. That we'd put it, her affair, behind us. Said we'd move on. That time was a great healer. Of course, I hated what she'd done, but could see that she was ashamed of herself. She assured me it would never happen again. Said the affair was a meaningless aberration. Everyone makes mistakes. I, for one, should have told you earlier about the events of Wednesday and Thursday. To my way of thinking, it's how we recognise, react and put things right afterwards, that define us as human beings. Claire is, was, a beautiful person. Yes, she messed up. But don't we all, sometimes?'

'I suppose we do, yes. Can I ask you a sensitive question, Mr Tomlinson?'

'You may.'

'The pathologist noted bruising to Claire's genitals and along the inside her thighs. It would suggest your love making on Sunday was vigorous. Would you agree?'

Tomlinson's face flushed scarlet. 'Inspector, Claire bruised easily. Don't ask me why, she just did.'

'I see. What did you do next?'

'I mooched around the garden, then delivered Emily to a friend's house at one. Claire made Sunday lunch and packed an overnight bag. We sat down to eat at half four. Claire left at six. She hates to let people down, especially Sally. I picked Emily up at half past seven. When we got home, we, Emily and I, had a quiet night. Around half eight, I emailed work telling them I was taking a couple of days off. I fancied some time on my own around the house doing odd jobs. I couldn't face being around people. I'd had a traumatic few days.'

'Monday and Tuesday, did you go anywhere in your car?'

'I dropped Emily at school in the morning, and picked her up in the afternoon, both days. I dropped her off at ten to nine each morning. Picked her up at half three each afternoon.'

'During Monday, were you drinking, Mr Tomlinson?'

A pause. 'Yes. I broke open a pack of lager. Drank two. It was a hot day, I was gardening. It was thirsty work. I wasn't drunk when I picked Emily from school, if that's what you're inferring. I was stone-cold sober. I would never drive under the influence, inspector.'

'I'm glad to hear it. The thing is Mr Tomlinson, Claire's sister, Ellie, said she spoke to you on Monday afternoon. She got the impression you'd been drinking. Said you were rather short with her. As you might expect, she was concerned about Claire.'

'Inspector, Ellie and me, don't get on. I put up with her for Claire and Emily's sake. She was mumbling something about Claire not arriving Sunday night. She was talking utter gibberish. I told her she'd probably got her dates mixed up. I assured her that Claire was in Masham with Sally. I admit I put the phone down on her. Ellie's a stirrer. I wasn't interested in what she'd got to say. When Claire's at Sally's, I try not to bother her. We never contacted one another when we're with friends. We respected one another's need for space. For example, my golfing trips are sacrosanct.'

'Mr Tomlinson, will your daughter be able to confirm that you didn't leave the house on Sunday night?'

'I would have thought so, yes. We watched a movie together. It was *Deadpool*. Not my usual kind of thing, but I enjoyed it. It's manic. Shall I get her?'

'That won't be necessary. We'll swab your mouth, download your phone data, and then we'll be off.'

'No problem. Anything that puts Boyd behind bars sooner rather than later, is fine by me.'

CHAPTER TWELVE

WEDNESDAY 9TH AUGUST, **4:00 p.m.**

The door into Owen Boyd's apartment swung open. Boyd stood in the opening, arms folded across his chest.

'Good afternoon, Mr Boyd.'

'Afternoon, gentlemen. To what do I owe the pleasure?'

'We'd like to discuss your relationship with Claire Tomlinson. I expect you know she's been murdered.'

'Yes, I heard on the local TV news. It's terrible. I'm heartbroken. Come in, gentlemen, I've nothing to hide.'

'Thank you.'

They settled in the sparse, contemporary-styled lounge.

'Can I get you something to drink?'

'We're fine, thanks. This won't take long,' Wardell replied.

'That's good to hear. So, what do you want to know?'

'We'd like you to describe your movements from late Friday night – after they threw you out of The Rose and Crown –

through to Monday morning. We'd like – with your permission, of course – to swab the inside of your mouth and make a copy of your mobile phone's sim card data. David, will do the honours. He's brought along the laptop. Happy, Mr Boyd?'

'I suppose I'm going to have to be, aren't I?'

'When you put it like that, I suppose you are, yes,' said Wardell, flatly.

'Am I under suspicion, inspector? I can assure you, I had nothing to do with Claire's murder.'

'It's fair to say that we are interviewing everyone connected to Claire Tomlinson. The fact is, Mr Boyd, the last time anyone saw you in public with Mrs Tomlinson, your emotions were, to put it mildly, running high. Eye witnesses say you manhandled her in the pub car park. You bruised her. You committed criminal damage.'

'I know. I behaved appallingly, Friday night. I'm ashamed of myself. I know it's no excuse, but I was pissed out of my brain. That said, my dreadful behaviour on Friday night, doesn't make me a murderer.'

'True enough. If you could describe your movements after Friday night, sir. David, take notes, please.'

'OK. As I've already mentioned, after the barney in the car park, I went for a kebab. I had takeaway. Ate it on the way home. I must've arrived home around half past midnight. I can't be sure, since I was three sheets to the wind. Saturday morning, I slept in until half eleven. When I woke up, I was still in my clothes. I'd ruined my best bloody shirt. Somehow, I'd got chilli sauce all down the front. I nipped downstairs and chucked it in the communal bin – Monday is bin day. After that, I made a fry-up. I wasn't feeling too good. There's nothing better than a greasy fry-up to help you get over a hangover. I must've downed going on for four pints of water. I felt much better afterwards. Saturdays, I play golf. That particular weekend I was taking part in a competition on Sunday. I was at a loose end. I went out for a walk to clear my head. To mull things over.'

'I take it you're referring to Mrs Tomlinson ending your relationship?'

'Yes, that's right. I was annoyed with myself for losing my rag. I'd let the drink get the better of me. I hate it when that happens. In my teens, I could drink anyone under the table. Nowadays, I'm a bloody lightweight. I'm drunk as a skunk on five pints of cheap lager. You don't want to know me when I'm on spirits.'

'Probably not,' mumbled Wardell. 'OK. Did you have any contact with Mrs Tomlinson, overnight on Friday?'

'No. None. Which only added to my frustration. I admit, early Saturday afternoon I sent two texts to Claire begging for forgiveness. She ignored both.'

'That must have been hard?'

'Inspector, you've no idea. Anyway, I kept walking. I ended up doing a five mile circular walk along country lanes; got back in Osmotherley around three. I couldn't resist a quick one in The Feathers. I bumped into an old school mate and we had ourselves a session – hair of the dog. I left The Feathers at quarter to six. As soon as I got home, I had a siesta. Woke up at half seven and ordered takeaway pizza. Whilst I was eating, I received a text from Teresa.'

'Teresa?'

'My fiancée. My *ex fiancée*, to be exact.'

'I see. And what did it say, Mr Boyd? This text from your ex, Teresa.'

'She asked if I'd like to meet up. It was obvious that she'd heard on the grapevine about the ding-dong I'd had with Claire, the night before.'

'And did you meet up?'

'Yes, we did.'

'I take it the split with your fiancée was amicable?'

'No. Don't ask me why she wanted to meet up. I can't fathom the female mind at the best of times. Only, she seemed concerned about me. I thought, what the hell? I had nothing to lose. I was at a loose end, anyway. I met her at the taxi rank in Osmotherley at half eight. We took a cab into Northallerton. At first, the conversation was strained. After we'd had a few drinks, things loosened up. It may seem weird, but we had a splendid night. I ended up staying over at her place.'

'You did?' said Wardell, unable to conceal his surprise.

'Yes, I did. Eh, I get it where and when I can, inspector. One never knows when the next bus will come along. I was at a low ebb. My ego needed a boost.'

'Bit cynical, don't you think?'

'Who cares? I don't.'

'OK. That takes us to Sunday morning.'

'Sunday morning, I took off from Teresa's place around ten'ish. She was fast on. The golf competition was teeing off at noon. It's not an option to be late for a golf competition.'

'How did your round go?'

'Awful. I felt exhausted. I kept getting double vision. I got home at six o'clock, laid on the couch, and had a power nap. An incoming text message from Claire woke me at about quarter to eight. She asked to meet up at Devil's Bridge at half eight.'

'Really? And you're familiar with Devil's Bridge?'

'Yes. Claire and I used to meet up at there for sex.'

'And did you go to Devil's Bridge?'

'I travelled there, yes. She stood me up. I tried her on her mobile, but all I kept getting was the "this mobile is switched off" message,' said Boyd, miming quotation marks.

'What time did you arrive at Devil's Bridge? I want you to be accurate, Mr Boyd.'

'Eight thirty. I remember checking the dashboard clock as I pulled into my usual spot against the pines.'

'And which vehicle did you use? The Aston?'

'No, I used the Range Rover. The Aston's no good on the lane leading up to Devil's Bridge. I didn't want to damage the suspension.'

'I see. And there was no sign of Claire or her silver BMW at Devil's Bridge?'

'No, none.'

'Did you hang around for long?'

'Best part of an hour.'

'Did you see anyone else during that hour?'

'Not a soul. A fox walked straight past me at one point. Bold as brass, it was.'

'Did you notice a mound of stones under the pines ten yards from the bridge?'

'I can't say that I did, no.'

Wardell ran a hand over his chin, scratched under his left ear, his forehead creased in thought. 'How did you feel when you realised you'd been stood up?'

'Empty. I wanted to get home, close the blinds, and watch mindless TV.'

'Is that what you did?'

'Yes. I gave it till half nine, thought sod this for a game of soldiers, and set off for home.'

Silence hung in the space between them. Wardell drew a long breath.

David Watts cleared his throat. 'Boss. DNA sample. Sim card.'

'Oh, yes, thank you for reminding me, David. Mr Boyd, would you mind providing a sample of DNA?'

'No problem. I've nothing to hide.'

'Mr Boyd, when you heard that someone had murdered

Claire at Devil's Bridge, given what you've just told us, didn't you think it would be a good idea to call the police?'

Boyd shrugged. 'To be honest, no. I assumed Claire was killed much later. Days, even. I didn't consider me being there was in any way relevant. When we first had a rendezvous at Devil's Bridge, I remember Claire telling me it was one of Drew's favourite places. I assumed Claire's head was all over the place. That she'd bottled seeing me. I thought I was best off out of it. She'd stirred up a hornet's nest with Drew. He had the perfect motive for murder, didn't he? Infidelity. It's not nice.'

'Oh, the bloody irony,' Wardell said under his breath.

'What did you say, inspector?'

'Nothing. OK. Your movements since Sunday, Mr Boyd?'

'I've been in the office all week holding the fort. The married men have been off on their jolly holidays. It's that time of year. Evenings, I spent here, at home, watching TV and chilling.'

Wardell had had enough. 'Over to you, David. Swab Mr Boyd's mouth and download the data from his phone. I'll be outside getting a breath of fresh air. There's a nasty smell in here.'

* * *

'What do you think?' Wardell asked Watts from the driver's seat.

'I don't know what to think. He's a shameless opportunist and an obnoxious bastard, that's for sure. I mean, how low can someone go, having it off with your ex just hours after splitting with your so-called "special one". If you ask me, him saying he texted Claire to meet up at Devil's Bridge is too convenient. It puts him at the locus around the time of the murder. Makes you wonder if he's trying the reverse psychology card.'

'It does. Let's get back to the ranch. Get those DNA swabs

over to Kenny G. Brief Bina to print out whatever's on their sim cards. Arrange for the service providers to come up with tracked locations for both of them, over the weekend. Ought to make interesting reading.'

CHAPTER THIRTEEN

David Watts gazed across Harrogate city centre from the conference room window. Four storeys below, a steady stream of traffic flowed past on the A59. Behind him, on the desk, sat six neat piles of A4 paper in two groups of three. The piles contained forensic reports, mobile phone sim card data printouts and tracked locations for both Drew Tomlinson's and Owen Boyd's mobile phones.

Overhead – despite the early morning heat – dark foreboding clouds scuttled across a grey sky. Liquid pebbles spat against the glass, as if catapulted by rowdy teenagers.

The door creaked open. Wardell bounded in and hurried over to the tea trolley.

'Coffee, David?'

'Don't mind if I do, guv. Ta.'

'Black?'

'Yes, guv.'

Wardell poured two cups of black coffee from the percolator, turned, made his way to the desk, set the cups down and leaned forward, studying the piles.

Without looking up, Wardell said: 'Sorry I'm late. I bumped into his bloody lordship. Just given me a right royal bollocking, he has. Nasty so-and-so. He's pissed off because I'm late with the monthly crime stats report. I'm bloody seething. There's not enough hours in the day as it is. Bloody admin. It drives me up the wall. Him and the PCC, they're wired to the bloody moon. Anyway, I see forensics and the phone companies have come good?'

'That's right, guv. Everything you wanted is right here.'

'Everything?'

'Yep. DNA results. Printouts of call registers, text messages, emails and tracked locations for Drew Tomlinson's and Owen Boyd's mobile phones for the period 28th July to 5th of August. Everything.'

'Excellent. Have you studied them?'

'I've had a brief look, yes. I couldn't contain myself. Hope you don't mind?'

'No, not at all. I was hoping you had, to help speed things up.'

'They make very interesting reading.'

'OK,' said Wardell, dragging out a chair, loosening his tie and plonking down. 'Let's get going. Time and tide and all that.'

Watts lowered into the chair next to Wardell and placed the palm of his right hand on the three piles relating to Drew Tomlinson.

'Tomlinson first, guv?'

'Go for it.'

'How much detail do you want?'

'Cut to the quick, David. His nibs wants his blasted report by five at the latest. Otherwise, he'll throw his teddy out of his pram, again.'

Watts smirked. 'I'll go slow, then.'

'Cheeky sod. Don't you dare.'

'OK. Forensics confirm the semen found in Claire Tomlinson at the time of her death was Drew Tomlinson's. As you know, that's consistent with him saying they'd had sex on Sunday afternoon. There's no evidence of his semen on the rug she was wrapped in. As expected, forensics recovered Tomlinson's DNA, fibres from his clothing and hair from inside the victim's BMW.'

'No surprise there, then. It's his wife's car, after all. I'm much more interested in the tracked locations of his mobile phone. Was he, from Sunday afternoon through to Tuesday night, anywhere near Devil's Bridge? A simple yes or no will suffice.'

'No. Saturday morning he was at home in Thimbleby. In the afternoon, he travelled to Helmsley. Saturday night the data suggests he was static in Helmsley. Sunday morning, he travelled home to Thimbleby. Phone records confirm he dropped Emily off at school in the mornings and picked her up, Monday and Tuesday afternoons. What's interesting are his movements Sunday, early evening.'

'Go on.'

'Remember he told us he picked Emily up from her friend's house in Osmotherley at 7.30 p.m.?'

'I do. Go on.'

'The timed and tracked locations of his phone suggest he followed Claire in her car from Thimbleby to within a hundred yards of Boyd's flat in Osmotherley. He'd set off from home shortly after she'd left, and followed her, keeping a safe distance at all times. CCTV captured him arriving, sat in his car, and departing at 6.45 p.m. He never got out of the car.'

'Really?'

'Yes. He never got out.'

'He never mentioned that, did he?'

'Nope. He never did.'

'How long was he in Osmotherley?'

'That's the thing, guv, not long. Just five minutes from 6.40 to 6.45 p.m. Seems he parked within a hundred yards of where she'd pulled up in the car park, outside Boyd's flat.'

'Sixty-four-million-dollar question is: where did he go after that?'

'I know exactly where he went and what he did.'

'You do?'

'I do. He drove himself to The Old White Bear at Elmsby, three miles east of Osmotherley, and sank three pints in just fifteen minutes.'

'You're sure?'

'Yes, guv, I drove there earlier. Talked to the landlord. He confirmed Drew Tomlinson was there from 6.55 p.m. to 7.10 p.m. Phone records show he drove from there to Emily's friend's house and picked her up at half seven. That part is consistent with his statement. I reckon he would have been over the limit, and that's the reason he never mentioned he'd followed Claire to Boyd's flat.'

'I think you're probably right. The poor sod will have been drowning his sorrows, I expect. He thought he'd been led up the garden path again. Her, going to see Boyd, in his flat.'

'Seems so, guv... Seems so...'

'Did he make any calls, send any texts and, or emails, to Claire, Monday and Tuesday?'

'Yes, guv. He called her on her mobile several times. She never returned his calls. Which isn't surprising given that someone had switched her phone off, and it was laying in the woods near to where she was found. He'd sent her several innocuous text messages asking her where she was over the course of Monday and Tuesday, without getting a reply.'

'Looks like he's in the clear, then?'

'I reckon so, guv. We're certain Claire Tomlinson was

murdered early Sunday evening. Tomlinson confidently suggested Emily could alibi him to the house all of Sunday evening and night.'

'Good. OK. What about the randy sod, Boyd?'

'Are you sitting comfortably, guv?' said David Watts with a broad grin.

'I am.'

'First things first. Forensics matched Boyd's DNA to the semen stains recovered from the rug she was wrapped in. I had Kenny visit Boyd's flat and take samples from the floors of each of the main rooms. He's analysed fibres recovered from the lounge in an area close to the kitchen door. Guv, they're a precise match to the rug. He's confident the match will stand up in court. Therefore, we've established a direct evidential link between the rug, the victim, and Boyd's flat.'

'Excellent work, David. That said, it's still not beyond a reasonable doubt Boyd murdered her, is it?'

'No, guv, you're right, it isn't. However, the phone records for Claire Tomlinson and Owen Boyd make interesting reading.'

'Tell me more.'

'They tracked Claire Tomlinson's phone to Boyd's flat. She arrived at 6.38 p.m. on Sunday. Tracked leaving at 6.48 p.m. She arrived at Devil's Bridge at 7.15 p.m. Boyd told us he arrived home at six and left for Devil's Bridge at 8.05 p.m. His statement corresponds to the tracked locations of his mobile. However, and it's a massive *however*, take a look at the text conversation between Boyd and Claire Tomlinson, guv. It started at 7.45 p.m. on Sunday. The first message being from Claire Tomlinson's mobile.'

Watts handed Wardell a sheet of A4 with a long list of text messages. A single text message highlighted yellow.

. . .

19:45

sorry for not getting back to you... missing you like crazy... I'm stupid... let's make up... tonight... like only we can... I'm here already... I luv u... sorrreeee... forgive me... come quick... not literally... C xxx

'Dated Sunday?' Wardell asked.

'Yes. Sunday the 30th July.'

'OK, correct me if I'm wrong, but it looks to me like she called at Boyd's flat and he didn't answer. He was probably asleep with the key in the door. She wouldn't have been able to get in. What's interesting is the wording. "Sorry for not getting back to you", and "I'm here already". It suggests there was prior communication and arrangement to meet up at Devil's Bridge.'

'I agree, guv. So, I did some digging.'

'OK. And?'

'And Scientific Support recovered a deleted text message from Boyd's mobile. The text was sent from his golf club at 3 p.m. on Sunday. They reconstructed it for our benefit.'

Watts handed Wardell a slip of paper.

15:00

desperate to see U... still hurting bad... hate what happened Friday... ashamed... was pissed... not proud... luv U & want U back... please come tonight Devil's Bridge at 8... please... please... love O xxx

·   ·   ·

'Well, well, well. Seems someone's been holding out on us, doesn't it, David?'

'It would seem so, yes, guv. Especially given that the rug she was wrapped in came from his flat. There's something else. Something significant.'

'Go on.'

'SOCO found semen on the front of the victim's jeans that were recovered from the crime scene. They were a perfect match against Boyd's DNA.'

'You're joking?'

'Nope, it's his alright. Also, there was a small quantity of Boyd's semen inside her.'

'It's time that we dragged Owen bloody Boyd in on suspicion of murder. Let forensics loose on his flat. I suspect they'll turn up even more conclusive evidence.'

'Fingers crossed, guv, I think there's every chance they will.'

CHAPTER FOURTEEN

Wardell collected the landline on the third ring and recognised Kenny Goddard's voice, instantly.

'Alan, I'm phoning with an update on the Tomlinson murder.'

'Oh, hello, Kenny. Good news, I hope. I could do with some.'

'Yes, Alan, the best. Your lottery numbers came up.'

'If only. What do you have for me, Kenny?'

'At some point, Alan, the rug and the victim's blood came into contact with the boot lining of the victim's BMW.'

'You're sure about that?'

'We are.'

'Excellent. That means someone used the victim's car to dispose of the body.'

'It does. I'm not through yet, Alan. Are you sitting comfortably?'

'I am.'

'As you know, we've conducted a thorough search of Boyd's flat using luminol and a cracking bit of kit we've just acquired which uses special UV light. I won't bore you with the technical details, but it worked a treat, first time out.'

'What did it come up with?'

'Blood spatter, Alan. Lots and lots of lovely, lovely, blood splatter.'

'Where from?'

'A sizeable area of the lounge floor next to the kitchen door. We recovered samples from the joints in the laminate flooring, the lower half of the door, and vertically along the architraves up to about a metre above floor level. You'll love me for the next part.'

'I love you already, Kenny, but you already know that.'

'Oh, that's so nice. I feel all warm inside.'

'And so you should.'

'Anyway, less of the love-in. The luminol identified a trail of blood to the unit beneath the kitchen sink. Inside the unit, wedged behind a false panel, we found a wheel brace. Back at the lab, we recovered hair and blood from the spanner end. You still there, Alan?'

'I am. I'm waiting with bated breath.'

'The hair and blood we found inside the spanner head are a DNA match to Claire Tomlinson's. Alan, I'm confident we found the murder weapon. I had someone drive down to the Land Rover dealership. A mechanic there confirmed the wheel brace as coming from the same model Range Rover owned by Boyd.'

'Kenny. I want your hand in marriage.'

'I'm flattered. I accept. On one condition. I get to choose the honeymoon.'

'You can, darling. Just not Skeggy. I've terrible memories of

Skegness. You and your team have done a sterling job, Kenny. Pass on my regards.'

'I will.' After a long pause. 'Nail the bastard, Alan. Poor woman suffered an awful death.'

'I will, Kenny. I will.'

CHAPTER FIFTEEN

Wardell and Watts stood with their backs pressed against the corridor wall outside the interview room, nonchalantly studying their phones.

Watts turned to Wardell. 'Long enough?'

Wardell shrugged. Checked the time on the wall clock. 'Nah, let them stew a little longer. You're going to have to learn to pace yourself, David. There's no point rushing in. You youngsters, you want everything doing yesterday.'

'Fair do's, guv,' said Watts, returning his attention to the phone, smirking. 'It's no skin off my nose.'

Ten minutes passed. Wardell lifted from the wall, pushed his phone deep into a trouser pocket, and collected an A4 hardback notebook from the floor.

'C'mon. I suppose we'd best crack on. By now, Manny will hot under the collar. Slimy bugger gets on my nerves. Work the tape and take notes. I'll do the talking. No point stepping on one another's toes. OK?'

'Fine.'

They pushed through the door and entered a small, window-less room furnished with a solitary desk, four chairs, recording equipment, and a single video camera hung on the wall below the ceiling. Owen Boyd sat next to his solicitor, Manny Cohen – a white-bearded, near octogenarian in a skullcap. The seated men rotated their gazes to the detectives.

Wardell and Watts lowered into the seats opposite. Cohen scowled, tapped his wristwatch and sighed. 'Life is like riding a bicycle, Alan. To keep your balance, keep moving forward. Did your mother never tell you that, Alan?'

'Can't say that she did,' said Wardell, setting the papers on the table, appraising Cohen through narrowed eyes. 'What's a matter, Manny? Miss breakfast? You seem a little tetchy.'

'You know perfectly well what's up, Alan. You've disre-spected myself and my client by keeping us waiting. You're fifteen minutes late. We're busy people. Neither of us appreciates being kept waiting. Your childish mind games haven't gone unnoticed.'

Wardell smirked. 'I'm sorry you think that, Manny. Impor-tant police business waits for no man. Isn't that right, David?'

'Yes, sir,' said Watts, grinning. 'It doesn't.'

Cohen shrugged, cast his arms wide. 'Eh, whatever. Now that you're here, can we please proceed? I've an important appoint-ment in Leeds at noon. I don't want to be late.'

Keep your hat on, thought Wardell, flicking open a notebook, scanning handwritten notes. 'I'll be brief. David, switch on the tape.'

'Righto, guv.'

Wardell cleared his throat. 'The date is Friday 11th August

2017. The time is 10.45 a.m. Those present include myself, Detective Inspector Alan Wardell, and Detective Sergeant David Watts of North Yorkshire Police Major Crime Unit. Also present are Mr Owen Boyd of 11 Ousethwaite House, Thimbleby, North Yorkshire and Mr Boyd's solicitor, Mr Manny Cohen. Mr Boyd, I'd like you to confirm you are attending this interview voluntarily.'

Boyd looked to Cohen. Cohen nodded.

'I can.'

'This interview is under caution. Mr Boyd, as a suspect in the murder of Mrs Claire Tomlinson, please confirm your acceptance of this.'

Manny dipped his head.

'I confirm my acceptance,' said Boyd.

'Mr Owen Boyd, you do not have to say anything, but it may harm your defence if you do not mention when questioned something which you later rely on in court. Anything you do say, may be given in evidence. Do you understand?'

'I do,' said Boyd, folding his arms across his chest.

'You are not under arrest.'

'Can we get on with it, inspector?' blurted Cohen, unable to contain his frustration any longer.

'All in good time, Manny, all in good time. This is a serious matter. A woman has been murdered. A married woman with a child. Someone with whom your client was having an affair. Someone who your client had a public altercation with less than forty-eight hours before she was killed.'

'I'm aware of my client's relationship with the deceased woman. If we could speed up, Alan.'

'Mr Boyd, I want you to summarise your movements on Sunday the 30th July of this year.'

'If I must. Although, for the record, I'd like it known, that I've been through this already in some detail several times.'

'I'm aware of that, Mr Boyd.'

'Mr Cohen?' asked Boyd.

'Go ahead. You have nothing to hide.'

Boyd cleared his throat. 'As I mentioned before, Saturday night I stayed over at my ex, Teresa Collins's flat. I left Teresa's place at ten o'clock Sunday morning. I understand you've already spoken to Teresa, and she has confirmed this.'

'We have.'

'I drove straight to the golf club. I tee'd off at midday. I had a shocking round. Got home just after six. I was knackered. I crashed on the settee. Had a nap. A text message from Claire woke me up at quarter to eight. She suggested we meet at Devil's Bridge. Asked me to get there quickly. I arrived at half eight, on the dot. Claire wasn't there. I assumed she'd got delayed. I gave it an hour. She never arrived. I was pissed off. When I got home, I made myself a sandwich, watched TV and went to bed.'

'And did you at any point on Sunday text Mrs Tomlinson?'

'No, I did not,' barked Boyd. 'I was too busy making a fool of myself on the golf course.'

'I see.' Wardell ran a finger down his notes. 'The killer disposed of Mrs Tomlinson's body in a rug forensically linked to your flat. It has your DNA on it, in the form of semen. How do you explain that?'

Boyd returned a blank expression, eyelids batting. He stalled. 'What colour was the rug? I've several rugs. I can't say I've noticed one missing.'

'Grey with black flecks.'

Wardell imagined the rapid rotation of cogs inside Boyd's head. Realisation dawned on Boyd's face. 'Oh, that one! I'm with you now. That's Claire's. She brought it over to the flat and put it at the bottom of the bed. She said it was a moving in present for me. I seem to recall she'd bought it from a mill shop out Pendle way. She said it went with the decor. We had sex on it. Christened it. Now that you come to mention it, the last time I recollect seeing it was Thursday night: the day before the ding-dong in the pub. It wasn't there over the weekend. I assumed Claire had taken it back on Friday, whilst I was at work. She still had a key. Whoever killed her must have found it in her car. It's the only logical explanation.'

'To the best of your knowledge, was the rug ever positioned anywhere else in the flat?'

Boyd frowned. Fifteen seconds passed. 'Yes. Claire tried it out first in the lounge beside the kitchen door. We decided it better suited the colour scheme in the bedroom.'

'I see. Mr Boyd, I'm going to ask you a specific and personal question. I'd like the courtesy of an honest and accurate reply.'

'Inspector, I hope you're not insinuating that my client is a liar?'

'Not at all, no. I'm emphasising the importance of your client's response.'

'OK, inspector, ask away,' said Boyd. 'At the risk of repeating myself, I've absolutely nothing to hide.'

'When did you last have sex with Claire Tomlinson? By sex, I mean full penetrative sexual intercourse.'

'Wednesday evening at the flat. At that point, Claire told me she was leaving Drew for good. Since we were celebrating, I cracked open a bottle of champagne. We drank it on the balcony and retired to the bedroom around nine thirty.'

'OK. And what was Mrs Tomlinson wearing that evening?'

'Wearing?'

'Yes, wearing. What was Claire Tomlinson *wearing* when she arrived at your flat on the Wednesday evening, before she disappeared on the Sunday?'

'Oh, I see. I assumed you meant was she wearing saucy underwear?'

'No.'

'I seem to recollect she was wearing a long, white summer

dress. Yes, that's right. It was white with red flowers. She looked stunning.'

'Was she wearing jeans?'

'No, inspector, she wasn't. It was scorching hot. When we sat on the balcony, it must've been in the low twenties even at that late hour.'

'Mr Boyd, I understand you own a Range Rover. Is that correct?'

'Yes, I do. I've owned Rangies for years. Any reason you ask?'

'How long have you owned this particular car?'

'This one, about three months.'

'During that time, did you have any reason to use the spare wheel, or the wheel brace?'

'I can't say that I have. So far, it's been utterly reliable.'

'Mr Boyd, your wheel brace is missing. Usually, it's located in the boot underneath the carpet. We checked. It isn't there.'

'OK. Is it relevant? It might have been misplaced at the dealership?'

'Mr Boyd, our Scene of Crime Officers, found the wheel brace hidden behind a false panel under the kitchen sink.'

Boyd interjected. 'Well, I didn't put it there if that's what you're implying.'

'Who else might have put it there?'

'I've no idea. All I know is that it wasn't me.'

Cohen cleared his throat. 'Is the wheel brace in any way associated with the crime you're so desperately trying to link my client with?'

Wardell nodded. 'Yes.'

'In what way?'

'SOCO recovered trace evidence in the form of Mrs Tomlinson's blood and hair from it. It was used to murder Claire.' Wardell paused. 'Mr Boyd, did you murder Mrs Claire Tomlinson?'

Cohen placed his gnarly fingered right hand atop Boyd's, leaned in and whispered into his ear. Boyd glowered at Wardell.

'No comment,' said Boyd.

'Final answer?' asked Wardell.

'No comment.'

Wardell sat back, closed his notebook, set it against his chest and leaned back in the chair. 'I'm ending this interview at 11.00 a.m. Stop the tape, please, Detective Watts. We too, are very busy men.'

ONE YEAR LATER

CHAPTER SIXTEEN

NORTH YORKSHIRE GAZETTE

JILTED OSMOTHERLEY MAN JAILED FOR MURDER OF THIMBLEBY WOMAN

Owen Boyd, 34, from Osmotherley, North Yorkshire, was today jailed for life for the brutal
murder of a married woman, Claire Tomlinson,
34. Mr Boyd is expected to serve a minimum
prison term of 30 years at a Category A prison.
Category A prisons are reserved for the most
serious of offenders.

A hill walker discovered the body of Claire
Tomlinson at Devil's Bridge — a beauty spot
two miles north of Osmotherley — on the
morning of 5th August last year. The police
forensically linked the body — wrapped in a

rug and hidden under a mound of stones — to Boyd's flat. Mrs Tomlinson received a significant blow to the back of the head. The inquest records the cause of death as drowning.

Leading the investigation, Detective Inspector Alan Wardell of North Yorkshire Police Major Crime Unit stated in court that compelling forensic evidence proved beyond reasonable doubt that Boyd was the killer. Inspector Wardell said after the jury reached their verdict, 'I'm delighted that Owen Boyd has been brought to justice for this particularly savage murder. There's no doubt in my mind that Claire Tomlinson survived the initial attack, only to be drowned by Boyd in the nearby beck. Boyd is a merciless, cold-blooded killer. My sympathy goes out to Mrs Tomlinson's husband, Drew, and daughter, Emily. They can start to rebuild their lives, safe in the knowledge that Boyd is where he belongs, behind bars.'

Sentencing Judge Owain Jones summed up by saying, 'The police investigation proved Mrs Tomlinson was subjected to a savage and cowardly attack by Boyd at his flat in Osmotherley. Afterwards, the body was transported in the boot of the victim's car to Devil's Bridge. Once there, Mrs Tomlinson regained consciousness. Without an iota of remorse, Boyd drowned her in the beck. Boyd killed Claire Tomlinson without mercy. This is a savage and heinous crime. I have no hesitation in passing down a full life term with a minimum tariff of thirty years.'

Mr Boyd's solicitor, Manny Cohen, commented: 'My client strenuously denies any involvement in the murder of Claire Tomlinson. He's innocent. He intends to appeal against the sentence and fight to put right this blatant miscarriage of justice. I have no further comment to make.'

Boyd starts his custodial sentence immediately.

40 YEARS LATER

CHAPTER SEVENTEEN

MONDAY 5TH AUGUST 2058 – **Seaview Care and Dementia Home for The Elderly, Beadnell Bay, Northumberland**

On-call GP, Maz Ahmed, rapped on care home manager May Cowan's, office door. He glanced at his wristwatch, ran a handkerchief over his sweated brow and sucked in a long and wearisome breath. He knocked again, flapped his shirt at the neck, seeking respite from the overbearing heat.

Maz heard a phone handset crash into the cradle, paper rustling, a window opening, and venetian blinds rattling.

'Come in,' called a female voice, in the softest of Geordie accents.

Maz pushed through the door and ambled to the desk. Cowan rose, offered a hand.

'How are you, doctor?'

'Harassed. Hot. Bothered. Overworked. Getting by.'

'Aye, it's hot all right. Hot weather's killed off all me plants, it has. Don't stand there on ceremony, doctor. Take the weight off. Sit yourself down.'

'Thank you.'

Dragging out a chair, the doctor lowered a well-worn leather satchel to the floor and sat down. Recovering a handkerchief, he wiped his forehead and pushed the moist square of cotton into a breast pocket.

'Water?' asked Cowan, rolling her gaze to the jug of iced water on the edge of the desk.

'Don't mind if I do.'

Cowan poured water into a tumbler and handed it across. The perspiring GP downed the water without coming up for air.

'Thank you. I needed that.'

'You're welcome. What can I do for you, doctor? I assume you are here to see Teresa Collins, in Room 15? She's been very ill.'

'I am. Mrs Cowan, I'm afraid the prognosis isn't good.'

'Aye, so they've been telling me. How long do you reckon she's got, doctor?'

Dr Ahmed drew a long breath. 'The cancer has spread to her lungs. According to her notes, she's Roman Catholic. Is that correct?'

'Aye, that's right. Everyone in rooms 10 through 20, are. It makes for ease of administration.'

'Mrs Cowan, you need to call a priest.'

'That close?'

'Yes. Best guess, six hours. It would surprise me if she makes it through the night.'

'I see. Shame. Teresa's a lovely woman. She's very popular with the fellas. Death comes to us all, I suppose. And 84, it's a fair inning by any standards.'

'It is,' said Ahmed, rising, reaching for the satchel. 'I'm sorry,

Mrs Cowan, I must be going. School holidays. We're short-staffed.'

'Aye, I expect you are. Thank you for coming, doctor.'

'No problem.'

Cowan stood. 'Can I see you out?'

'No, I'm fine,' said Ahmed at the door. 'Just make sure she takes her medication. She'll suffer otherwise.'

'I'll make sure of it. Thanks again, doctor,' said Cowan, reaching for the phone. 'Much appreciated.'

* * *

Roman Catholic priest, Seamus O'Dowd, entered Room 15, and stepped over to the bed. Stalling, he gazed down on Teresa Collins's wrinkled and emaciated face. Sinking onto a knee, O'Dowd settled The Holy Bible on the white cotton sheet and crossed himself.

Joining his hands, O'Dowd prayed.

Silence, but for the mucus rasps of Teresa's tortured breath against the low thrum of the air conditioning unit and the distant echo of children playing on the nearby beach.

O'Dowd collected Teresa's birdlike hand in his own. Her breathing quickened. Eyelids fluttered open. A vacant gaze met O'Dowd's. As the ember of life returned, Teresa sucked a long breath and made to push up. O'Dowd offered a calming hand and returned Teresa to the pillow.

'Settle down, child. The time has come, to rest.'

Consciousness flared and burned out.

Returned.

Rheumy eyes met O'Dowd's. 'Father. Confession.'

O'Dowd smiled. 'There's time, yet, child. Now, rest. Rest, while I pray. Pray for the redemption of your eternal soul.'

A quivering smile, eyelids sinking, resting breaths. 'Thank you, Father. You're right... Rest...'

O'Dowd settled the string of rosary beads against his cheek and murmured a stream of unintelligible syllables. Five minutes passed. Releasing Teresa's hand, O'Dowd spilled holy water over his fingers and made the sign of the cross on her clammy forehead.

Teresa startled awake, eyes flaring.

O'Dowd collected her hand. 'Teresa, it's time to confess your mortal sins. The doctor asked me here. My child, you haven't got long. Would you like to take confession?'

Gathering strength, Teresa fixed O'Dowd with a steel-blue gaze and drew breath.

'I would.'

'Good. Tell me, why did I come today, Teresa?'

'To hear my sins.'

'And have you sinned?'

'I have.'

'And when was your last confession?'

A long silence.

'A long time ago, Father.'

'How many years?'

'Forty.'

'That's a long time, my child. Is there anything weighing on your soul?'

'Yes, Father. The heaviest burden of all.'

'The heaviest burden of all?'

'Yes.'

'Would you like to confess this burden?'

'I would.'

O'Dowd quietened. A silent minute passed. 'Unburden yourself, Teresa. Confess your mortal sins.'

'Water, Father?'

O'Dowd poured water into a plastic cup, set it against Teresa's cracked lips. Tilting Teresa's head, he let her sip from the cup.

'Thank you,' she said, settling against the pillow, hollow gaze rising to the ceiling.

'This burden, Teresa. Why don't you tell me about it?'

A knowing smile morphing to a smirk, and with a shake of the head she confessed. 'Forty years ago, Father, I killed a woman.'

'Go on.'

'Her name was Claire Tomlinson. I drowned her.'

O'Dowd sat back, folded his arms across his chest, breathed deep and exhaled. 'Tell me, everything.'

'I killed her because she stole my fiancé, Owen. She sullied everything. Stole our future. Destroyed it all. I *had* to do something. So, I made a plan. Worked it out. Planted things. Made it look like *he'd* done it, my ex, Owen Boyd. I didn't care. I was past caring. Life wasn't worth living without Owen. I got away with it. They sentenced him to life in prison. He couldn't deal with the shame. Hated prison life. Just a year into his sentence, he hung himself. That was thirty-nine years ago. I did *everything* right. I outwitted them all. It was the perfect murder. I planted her blood, his semen, the murder weapon. I even stole things from his flat. I timed it all to perfection. I did everything to make it look like he'd done it. Stole things from his car. I even went to his golf club and text her using his phone to make sure she'd be where I wanted her to be, when I wanted her to be there. I killed her at their special place. The place I'd seen them. What they didn't realise was, I had keys made for everything: his flat, car, golf club locker, *everything*. I had copies made as soon as I suspected he was cheating on me. I'd only told him so much about my past. Betrayal scars you for life. It had happened to me before. The hurt lasts eternally. The thing is, Father...'

'Go on.'

'I don't feel guilt. Even now, as I'm confessing this greatest of all sins, I just feel numb, hollow, dead inside. Just like I did when I found out he was screwing someone.'

O'Dowd drew a breath. 'Hmm...'

O'Dowd stood, turned and stepped over to the window. There, he twisted the louvre blinds and opened the window. Sunlight flooding in. Cool air ran over his face. He stood breathing hard, savouring the air, enjoying the warm sun.

He waited and wondered, gazed at the perfect azure sky, considered eternity, man's inhumanity to man. Wondered if it would ever end. Doubted it ever would, or could. As a desperate forlorn weariness overcame him, he expelled the deepest of sighs.

He turned, looked across to the bed.

Teresa Collins lay with her mouth agape, lifeless eyes addressing the ceiling, drool spilling from the corner of her mouth, dark heart no longer beating.

THANK YOU!

I hope you enjoyed reading **MURDER AT DEVIL'S BRIDGE** as much as I enjoyed writing it. If you did, we would be forever grateful if you could take a moment to leave a review on your preferred platform.

Reviews help other people find our books and help us keep writing. We love hearing from readers. You can contact us via our facebook page, K W Cosgrave Author, or via our website. Here's the link to our **WEBSITE**.

www.indiumbooks.com

ABOUT THE AUTHOR

Keiron Cosgrave has written four crime novels and one novella. He has also co-written two further crime novels with his partner in crime and life, Christine Hancock.

This is Keiron's first novella under the Indium Books imprint.

Keiron lives in Yorkshire with partner Christine and has two grown up sons, Oliver & Louis. Keiron loves writing, reading, scooters and fair weather fishing.

ALSO BY KEIRON COSGRAVE

NOVELS

Promises, Promises

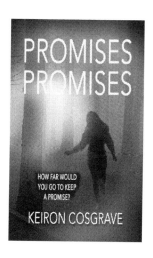

How far would you go to keep a promise?

After Kate and best friend Rose take revenge on their abuser at boarding school, their lives become macabrely connected forever.

Years later, Kate's father reveals decades old secrets. The veneer of middle-class respectability fractures. A childhood promise is stretched to breaking. A family implodes.

When Kate's father is found murdered, DI Alan Wardell unravels a complex web of desire, betrayal and greed. More family members are murdered...

Will Wardell catch the brutal serial killer before Kate becomes his next victim?

A roller coaster ride of raw emotion, which builds towards a breath-taking climax.

With Menaces

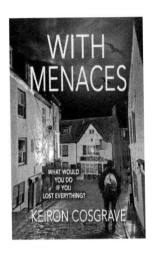

What would you do if you lost everything?

Cast on the scrap heap by his employers, pitied and despised by his soon-to-be ex-wife, Gavin Clark starts to lose his mind.

Homeless and hungry, Gavin gets caught up in the seedy underworld of a bleak seaside town at the end of the line.

As he descends in the abyss, Gavin hatches a sinister scheme to heap revenge on those he believes have wronged him.

He becomes a vigilante on the wrong side of the law.

Can Wardell untangle the dark psychology and motives of a vengeful and elusive serial killer, before more lives are destroyed?

A powerful story of hate, anger and revenge...

Beyond Absolution

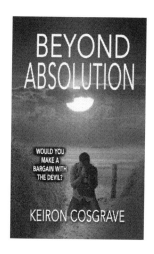

They thought the past was dead and buried...

A teenage affair in a church run boarding school attracts the wrath of priests and nuns... A pregnancy prematurely ended... A crime hushed up... A bargain made...

Years later, a suicide prompts disturbing allegations of historic sex abuse to surface...

A series of mysterious murders of boarding school friends...

Only one remains...

Wardell investigates the heinous decades old crimes and races to outwit a serial assassin before unholy secrets are taken to the grave...

A darkly compelling, yet ultimately heart-warming story of love, power and conspiracy, which will enthral and entertain the reader, to the final paragraph...

The Celtic Cross Killer

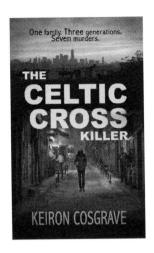

One family. Three generations.

Seven murders.

It is January 2005. New York is blanketed by snow. A killer driven by hatred roams the streets of Brooklyn.

Brooklyn pizzeria owner Ernest Costa leads a normal life. His business is thriving. He has a beautiful wife, and everything to live for. Returning home from work one freezing night, his life is snuffed out by a brutal and frenzied knife attack in a dark alley. His throat is slashed. A Celtic cross is slit deep across his back. Is the cross the signature of a psychopath? A recidivist who will strike again? Or is it an isolated attack? Someone knows the killer's identity...

Two years pass. The murder investigation stalls. Fingers are pointed at the senior detectives leading the manhunt. Removed from the case by his superiors, disgruntled NYPD Detective Antonio Pecarro decides to leave the force he once loved. He resigns and sets up as a private investigator.

Another body defiled with the same signature is discovered within sight of the victim's home. The victim's wife witnesses the killer leaving the scene. The killer's modus operandi is identical. Both victims are of Italian American heritage, of similar age and social standing. Is there a deranged serial killer driven by a compulsion to kill and bad blood walking the streets? Someone who will stop killing only when they are captured?

The investigation is re-launched. Criminal Psychologist Gerard Tooley is brought in. Progress is anaemic. Tensions bubble. Tooley is 'cut-free' from the team to pursue his own lines of investigation. Progress is made...

The heartbroken wife of the second victim decides to take matters into her own hands. She commissions P.I. Antonio Pecarro to identify and apprehend her husband's killer.

Another murder striking at the heart of the NYPD happens...

Will Pecarro solve the riddle before the NYPD and catch the serial killer before he strikes again?

The Celtic Cross Killer is a complex fast-paced historical crime thriller with a twist that will keep the reader guessing until its breath-taking climax.

Not Mine To Take

What if your hopes and dreams become your worst nightmare?

When bestselling novelist Erin Moran discovers her husband's infidelity, the threads holding together her life, ten-year marriage and career, start to unravel.

Under pressure from her agent and best friend, Olivia Pope, to rewrite her rejected latest novel, Erin seeks sanctuary on Scalaig – an idyllic tidal island on the west coast of Scotland.

Broken and depressed, with only her faithful golden retriever Bella for company, Erin settles in for a summer of renewal at her beloved Scalaig Lodge. What starts out as an escape soon becomes something far more sinister.

The locals in the nearby town of Scaloon, seem resentful of her presence, and Erin can't understand why?

Alone and isolated, cut off from the mainland twice a day, Erin's imagination runs wild.

Are the rumours of kidnap and murder the stuff of legend perpetuated to scare away strangers and interlopers? Or is Erin being warned off?

After a series of unexplained events, Erin questions her sanity...

Is someone out there? Is someone watching her every move? Is someone biding their time?

Not Hers To Take

All lives are precious. Are some lives more precious than others?

Ruby Harper is lost...

Betrayed by the man she loves, ostracised by her wealthy mother and high-flying sister, Ruby runs away to a world populated by drug users and abusive men.

When her mother dies prematurely, Ruby finds the strength to rebuild her shattered life and start anew.

But life is never that simple... Ruby has something precious... Something people want...

Who can she trust?

Her sister? Her best friend? Her lover?

Who stands to gain the most from Ruby's death?

For more information, visit our website:

www.indiumbooks.com

Or my Facebook author page - K W Cosgrave Author

Printed in Great Britain
by Amazon

78629114R00066